THE LITTLE BLUE BOOK ON

Krishna

DR SHUBHA VILAS

PRAKASH

Reprint 2024

PRAKASH

An imprint of Prakash Books India Pvt. Ltd

113/A, Darya Ganj,
New Delhi-110 002
Email: info@prakashbooks.com/sales@prakashbooks.com

Fingerprint Publishing
@FingerprintP
@fingerprintpublishingbooks
www.fingerprintpublishing.com

Copyright © 2021 Prakash Books India Pvt. Ltd

ISBN: 978 81 9491 650 5

Dedication

This book is dedicated to Dr. Niranjan Maniar,
a gentle, noble, and compassionate soul
who lived his life as a true Karma Yogi.

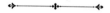

Introduction

Krishna is the God of love. He is known as Rasaraaj, which means the king of mellows. He is the king of relationships. Every person that connects with Him feels complete in their relationship with Him. There is no one in this world that can love like Him. There is no one in this world as lovable as Him. He was the best friend, the best son, the best lover, the best caretaker, and the best personality that graced this world. He sang and danced His way into people's hearts.

This book is a pandora's box of sweetness. Here, you will find such delightful stories of Krishna's interactions with all His near and dear ones that you will drown in that sweetness filling your heart with love and joy. Every story in this book will send you reeling just as you would after consuming huge quantities of gulab jamun (sweet paneer balls dipped in sugar syrup). These stories will satisfy your very soul.

Each story in this book is written in a different voice, making the reading even more interesting. Each story involves various individuals connected to Krishna's life and is an auto-biography of prominent characters narrating their personal experiences with Krishna. These personal accounts add assorted flavours of their intimate transactions with Krishna. Some voices are soft, while some are harsh, some are loving, while some are angry, some voices are neutral, while some voices are childish, and yet others are mature. But every voice entertains us, enlightens us, and educates us about Krishna.

It's amazing because some tales are from the mouths of demons who were annihilated by Krishna. And yet, isn't it surprising that even demons had a very special bond and an unforgettable connect with Krishna?

This book is an anthology that beautifully weaves the multi-faceted and multi-hued personality of Krishna.

A few stories in this book are based on *Srimad Bhagavatam* and other scriptural epics, while most others have been sourced from elderly Vrajvasis who lived their lives in Vrindavan, the land of Krishna. The purpose of this book is to simply help you love Krishna more. If you are looking for an authentic rendition of Krishna's life then I highly recommend you to dive into the pages of Krsna - the Supreme Personality of Godhead by HDG A.C. Bhaktivedanta Swami Srila Prabhupada.

The stories span Krishna's life and explore aspects of His life that are unique to Him, giving you an insight into why He always wore the peacock feather, why He played the flute, how He obtained the Kaustubha jewel, the Sudarshan chakra and the Panchajanya conch. In fact, each possession that decorates Krishna's persona shares its own story.

I believe that you may not have heard many of these exciting tales before. Even if you have, it would probably be without the intricate details highlighted in this book. Krishna is known as "Anubhav Pradhan" which means that He came into this world to give us an experience of the spiritual world. His pastimes are orchestrated in such a way that you will simply become enthralled with Him. I invite readers to helplessly fall in love with the charming God of love and relationships, Krishna.

Contents

CHAPTER 1

Vasudeva:
SUCCESS AGAINST ALL ODDS

The last nine years of my life have been the harshest and yet, unbelievably, the most blessed ones. Of course, if anyone hears my story without seeing it from my perspective, they will surely feel those were the most cursed nine years in human existence by any measure. Which is why hearing this saga in my voice is so very important.

It all began on the day of my marriage. It was the happiest day of my life, which turned into the most dreaded day of my life. But in hindsight, when I reflect on that day, it was actually a happy day. Of course, while I was in the midst of my dreaded moment, it didn't seem that way. Gargacharya, the *kula* guru of the Vrishni dynasty to which I belong, orchestrated the happiness of that day. Kamsa, the prince of the Yadu dynasty, to which my wife Devaki belonged, sponsored the dread of that day.

When Gargacharya proposed the suggestion of my marriage with Devaki, my father, King Surasena, requested him to bring up the alliance in the court of Ugrasena, the king of the Vrishnis. My father was pretty sure that no king in this world could ever reject an alliance that the most revered Gargacharya brought up. And obviously Gargacharya had done his due diligence before even suggesting this alliance. It was not just diplomatic considerations that were thought of but even accurate astrological consultations were made to arrive at this conclusion. Devaki was the daughter of King Ugrasena's brother, Devaka. Ugrasena and Devaka were only too pleased with our alliance and the marriage date was fixed immediately.

The happiness of the family and of the citizens of both the kingdoms grew bountifully. Their joy was obvious in the way they were participating in the marriage celebrations. They danced and sang as if it was their own family wedding. I was so thrilled to see their joy. After all, the royalty lives only to keep the subjects happy and prosperous. In fact, everyone in both the families was so happy with the marriage ceremony that all differences and formalities were forgotten in a spirit of togetherness that is seldom seen in heavily formal royal weddings.

Then the most unexpected thing happened. Kamsa, the prince of Mathura and the most powerful person in that kingdom, volunteered to drive our chariot. He loved his cousin-sister Devaki so much that he dropped his royal pride and took on a driver's role as an expression of that love.

My gorgeous wife Devaki's eyes welled up with love, seeing her brother do this for her. The world was amazed at her otherwise cruel and destructive brother's constructive contribution to make our marriage ceremony even more memorable. Everyone knew that Kamsa was systematically making allies with the most powerful demons from every corner of the world. Mathura had recently witnessed the entry and exit of the cruellest, and more so, the ghastliest-looking demons at odd hours of the night. Everyone knew that Kamsa was planning something big, very big, with the help of his badass friends. But traces of humanity, even in Kamsa, were always a welcome change. However, that exhibition of humanity didn't last beyond a block from where the chariot procession had begun.

Suddenly, there was a massive thunderclap that jolted everyone into silence. The loud music, rattling of wheels, singing, and gossip—everything came to an eerie halt. There were no dark clouds and yet the thunderclap was deafening. Everyone looked skywards, almost expecting the sky to fall! The horses neighed and jumped around uncontrollably as if they were able to sense some powerful force that was confusing them. A disembodied voice from the skies spoke in a clear and loud voice for everyone to hear. "Kamsa! You fool! The eighth child of your sister Devaki is going to be the cause of your death. Without knowing this, you foolishly drive her chariot. Prepare for your imminent death!"

I could see the colour fading away from my brother-in-law's face. Mixed emotions began to play on the board of his pale face. He seemed angry, scared, upset, frustrated, confused, traumatised, sad, and insulted, all at once. He seemed to be a melting pot of emotions. He wanted to run away from the thousands of prying eyes and hide himself somewhere till he figured out everything that was happening seemingly all of a sudden. Yet, another side of him wanted to stand and fight against any force that dared to oppose him even if it was just a loud voice.

Suddenly, he decided to do something that I never expected in my wildest imagination. Dropping the reins of the horses, he pulled out his sword.

Holding the neck of my wife in his other hand, he raised his sword placing it right at the point where her head met her torso. I immediately understood the plan of my cruel brother-in-law. He was about to slaughter his own sister publicly on the day of her marriage. I could understand his dilemma very clearly. He could do nothing to harm the disembodied voice since he had no idea who it was. He could do nothing to harm the eighth child, who wasn't even born. The only person he could harm was the one who was chosen to be the instrument of his fall.

I had to do something to save Devaki. She was my responsibility now. Barely minutes ago, I had taken my marriage vows, one of which was the lifelong responsibility to protect her. While I was thinking very hard for a brainwave to handle the calamity that had struck us all of a sudden, I saw my pretty wife's face. I was surprised to see her smiling in spite of the sharp sword being held at her neck. That's when I realised that my wife was not just beautiful but intelligent, too.

In the midst of a highly negative situation, she was able to see a thin line of positivity to meditate upon. There was no fear, no anger, no confusion, and no strain. Just a smile of hope! Hope that her eighth child was going to be special. Just seeing her smile made me smile. I was able to see a glimpse of the Supreme Lord at the end of the dark tunnel into which we were being shoved. Probably, Devaki was able to see that glimpse even more clearly since she was, after all, the chosen one.

I understood that while Devaki was meditating on the future, it was my duty to focus on the present. While the future seemed bright, the present seemed dark. The future was the eighth child but the present was Kamsa. Through my years of diplomatic training, I realised that the best way to enter someone's heart was through words of praise. In the gravest of situations, respectful praise can help you achieve what fuming anger cannot. "O King, O my brother-in-law, you are the pride of our family. How is it that the most powerful warrior of our times, who has single-handedly defeated the most powerful superpowers of this world, is eager to kill a weak woman? When you yourself refused to fight Putana simply because she was a woman, how can you now kill your own sister? What will the world think about your contradictory actions?"

My comments made him think and his grip on Devaki's head loosened a bit. Since my words were having some effect, I continued to explain to him the temporary nature of this world and the temporariness of life itself. I wasn't sure how much my words were impacting my brother-in-law, but I could see that all the citizens who were standing around us were deeply affected and connected to my thoughts. His anger seemed to subside for a while but then I noticed it was on the rise again. I had to rethink my strategy. I needed to do something drastic that could save my wife's life.

In the midst of my epic dilemma, I promised something that no other father in the history of mankind would have ever promised. I said, "O Kamsa, your fear is from the eighth child and not Devaki. I promise you at this very moment that I will personally hand over every child that is born to us. Once the child is in your hands, you may choose to do what you like with the child. By dint of this promise, you have nothing to fear from Devaki now, or from her children in the future."

That seemed to convince Kamsa, who dropped his sword, jumped off the chariot, and walked away. The marriage procession continued but the pomp and joy were no longer there. Everyone walked but there was no gait. As soon as we reached home, Kamsa's army followed and surrounded the palace. It seemed my brother-in-law was just too disturbed and had sent the army to keep us under house arrest as an additional safety measure over and above my promise.

In exactly a year from that day, Devaki gave birth to a beautiful baby boy whom we lovingly named Kirtimaan. We wanted this child to become famous and hence the name Kirtimaan. But we knew in our hearts that his fame would last only for a day. With a heavy heart, I requested Devaki to hand over our child to me. She became hysterical with the very thought. She clung to our baby. With great effort, I somehow managed to convince her to let go of our first child. I couldn't bear to hear the sounds of a mother's wailing. I quickly ran out of our palace with the baby in my arms and a torrent of tears gushing out of my eyes.

When I offered the first child to Kamsa, he

was surprised. He seemed very impressed that I had decided to keep my promise, that without any reminder or force, had duly submitted the child. As a gesture of kindness and appreciation, he decided to let go of this child, as this wasn't really his target enemy.

Though I was the happiest father at that point in time, I knew that this happiness wouldn't last as the kindness in the mind of a wicked person seldom lasts. But if nothing else, this would give Devaki a few more moments of happiness with her child. While I was busy enjoying those unexpected moments of joy in the company of my wife and our first child, Kamsa had a surprise visitor who convinced him that the first child could be the eighth child and the eighth child could be the first child when seen in a cyclic manner. The moment Kamsa was swayed into believing that the language of the gods couldn't be trusted, he rushed into my palace. He had, by then, mentally convinced himself that everyone's words were deceptive, including mine. He rushed into Devaki's bedroom. She was so happy to see her brother visit us. Little did she realise the sinister motive behind it.

In a moment, Kamsa grabbed the child from the hands of Devaki and, without a second thought, he flung the baby across the room, dashing him against a wall. All that was left of our first child was the blood splattered across the wall. Devaki and I were speechless. The shock was so numbing that we couldn't even cry. Unable to handle the shock, we collapsed on the floor.

On returning to consciousness, we found ourselves shackled with iron chains, locked inside a dark prison house. It took us days to come to terms with what had happened to us. While we were recovering from the shock, we heard more and more bad news. Kamsa had revolted against the present king Ugrasena, his own father, and had usurped the kingdom declaring himself the new king. As the situation of the kingdom turned bad to worse, both of us decided to focus on something that was destined. We knew that there was nothing we could do externally. The only thing we could do was to help fulfil the prophecy somehow.

With great faith, we kept having children every year. No sooner than the baby was born, Kamsa would walk in and ruthlessly kill our offspring right in front of our eyes. In this way, we lost six precious children. Our pain was expanding but along with that, so was our hope.

When it was time for the seventh child to be born, a miracle happened which no one was able to fathom at that moment in time. At some point in the pregnancy, the seventh child in the womb of Devaki suddenly disappeared. While we were confused then, we were later told by the great seers that the child was transferred from the womb of Devaki to the womb of Rohini, who was also my wife residing in the safety of Vrindavan, miles away from Kamsa's atrocities. Of course, the disappearance of the pregnancy caused great confusion in Kamsa's mind. He had no idea if this child who disappeared was to be counted. The nurses declared it to be a miscarriage.

Many months passed in this confusion for Kamsa and us. While we waited for the eighth child to be born to Devaki, I was informed that Rohini had given birth to a beautiful baby boy in Vrindavan in the house of my friend Nanda. Though I couldn't see our seventh child, I was secretly told about his beauty and charismatic personality. Immediately after that, numerous mystical things began to happen to us daily. We initially felt we were dreaming or even hallucinating. But then later, when we realised that Devaki was pregnant with the eighth child, we observed more obvious and clear signs of mystical beings around the prison cell all the time. It all began one day when I felt a divine presence in the region of my heart. It felt so special and overwhelming. All of a sudden, I felt something shoot from my heart and enter into the heart of Devaki. From her heart, a special glow travelled downwards and settled itself cosily in her womb. Devaki suddenly began to experience all the symptoms of pregnancy. For the first time in those eight years, we were filled with a feeling of fearlessness. Something seemed to be telling us that we need not worry anymore. Devaki was glowing. In fact, the entire prison cell radiated with her effulgence.

Kamsa's men rushed to inform him about the happenings in the cell. Kamsa was petrified. When he came to see us, we could see the same fear in his eyes that we saw when in the chariot that day. He very well knew his time was up. His mind was engulfed in fear and no solution seemed to be in sight. He chose to move away from the presence of Devaki and prepare himself for the inevitable. While time was ticking away, Devaki and I were relishing every moment of those eight months that the pregnancy lasted. Every single day we could feel the presence of divine beings inside the prison cell. Though we never saw anyone, we heard voices that sounded like prayers.

One day, there was a series of changes in the atmosphere heralding auspiciousness. The ten directions became pure. Divine sounds echoed from all directions. The low rumbling of victory drums could be heard even inside the prison cell. Clouds showered rain in great joy.

In such an auspicious atmosphere, right in the middle of the night, in that dense dark prison cell, the eighth child, who was the Supreme Personality of Godhead, appeared from Devaki just like a sacrificial fire appears automatically from *arani* wood by the auspicious chanting of mantras.

As I gazed at the newborn child, my jaw dropped. Right in front of me was my bundle of joy. Unbelievably beautiful. The dark-hued baby was kicking his two little legs in the air. His dark limbs were so delicate, soft like fresh butter. Surprisingly, he was fully decorated with ornaments at birth itself. Not just that, he was born with four arms, each holding a conch shell, a disc, a mace, and a lotus. The most captivating was his smile. The moment I saw that smile, I was overcome with one thought. The eight odd years of trauma that we faced was worth it just to be able to see that smile. That smile brought great solace to the bruised and broken heart of a father who had lost six children. The whole experience of drowning in the beauty of the tiny tot was so divine that I had completely forgotten my whereabouts. I fell on my knees and mentally offered millions of cows in charity.

By then, Devaki had woken up from the slumber of labour pain. Together, we offered heartfelt prayers to the Supreme Lord who was born as our son. Right after that, the mother's heart took over. Devaki began to express her concern for the safety of the child. She begged him to transform himself to look like a regular human child so that Kamsa did not suspect anything.

The little boy surprisingly began to speak to us. In a very sweet voice, he reassured us of protection and advised us not to worry about Kamsa's atrocities henceforth. In fact, he instructed me to carry him across the Yamuna river to Vrindavan and exchange him for Nanda's daughter, who was just born to Yashoda. Next, he transformed himself into a normal human child with two arms and dressed in no clothes. Devaki's joy knew no bounds when she saw a normal child in her arms. She immediately began to feed him her milk, her liquid love.

As soon as I held the divine baby in my arms, my shackles fell apart. The prison door swung open. The guards were knocked unconscious on the floor. I walked out with the little child in a basket. As soon as I stepped out of the prison cell, a torrential downpour greeted me. I continued walking, braving the rains and the heavy winds, shielding my little child from the raging elements.

As I reached the Yamuna river, something mystical happened. A huge serpent with a thousand hoods began to glide behind me, providing an umbrella to shelter the little boy in that basket. My child thrust out one of his feet, dangling it outside the basket. Just then, a wave from the river leaped high and touched the soft little foot of my child. The moment that happened, the Yamuna river parted and created a path for me to walk across to Vrindavan. I rushed into Nanda Bhavan, making sure that no one saw me. Some divine force guided me directly into the bedroom of Yashoda. There, my friend Nanda's wife was lying unconscious after labour pain. Next to her was the most beautiful baby girl that I ever saw. As instructed, I quietly placed my little bluish-black boy next to Yashoda and picked up the golden girl-child and tiptoed out.

As I made my way back to the prison cell of Kamsa, everything returned to normal once again. The guards woke up from their stupor. The chains fastened themselves to my limbs. The prison cell doors auto-locked. The baby girl timed everything to perfection. As soon as things were back in order, the baby girl began to cry. Kamsa was immediately informed. He rushed in with great anger. He had been anticipating this child for a long time now. He had to act quickly. But imagine his shock when he saw that the eighth child was a baby girl. He was flabbergasted at the thought of his death predicted at the hands of a girl. His male ego was too disturbed by that idea. Nonetheless, he had to do the needful.

With the practice of the six children he had killed already, Kamsa effortlessly picked this little baby by her legs and swung her expertly to crush her on the very wall where the bloodstains of her older brothers were still grossly visible.

However, even before he could release her from his grip, the baby girl slipped out of his hands. Assuming the form of a beautiful goddess seated on a thousand-petal lotus, she addressed Kamsa. She warned him that his time was up and the eighth child whom he had been waiting for had already been born elsewhere. In time, he would come and put an end to Kamsa's atrocities. The sight of the divine goddess shook Kamsa to the core. He suddenly became compassionate and sensible. He realised that he had unnecessarily been troubling us. The eighth child was born elsewhere. He released us from the prison after eight long years and ceremoniously sent us back to our palace. Our life of misery ended thus. But a life of hope began elsewhere.

CHAPTER 2

Putana:

PAGES FROM THE LAST DAY
OF MY MEMOIR

My name is Putana. I am also called Bala-ghatini because I specialise in killing children and I love my job. People also call me Khechari because I am a witch who can fly in the sky, mounted on a stick. My dishevelled appearance, which many of my friends often joke about, was not too different from that of a mendicant. I had matted locks of long hair that were in disarray. Except for that, I had nothing in common with the weak mendicants. My razor-sharp teeth were perfectly suited and adapted for biting babies. My lips were thick and huge. My eyes were socketed and looked like a pathway and my eyelashes resembled the hoods of a snake. My greatest weapons were my two breasts that brimmed with the most lethal poison that could finish babies in a moment. I could devour children like humans eat rice. King Kamsa considered me to be his sister. Although he had originally come to kill me, he decided to befriend me when he saw my superwoman prowess. Aware that I was the daughter of Maharaj Bali, the king of the demons, Kamsa knew of my demonic nature and how he could utilise it effectively to further his cause.

The call from Kamsa came one night. He was not his usual self. He was overcome by great fear and he trembled as he spurted out his instructions. I was ordered to kill every baby that was born in the last ten days in and around Mathura district. It was probably one of the best days of my life because I was getting to do what I loved the most and with no restrictions whatsoever. What I didn't realise at that time was that it was also going to be the last day of my life!

I knew that Nanda, the king of Gokula, had an invincible arrow in his possession that was famously called the arrow of Narayan. We demons stood no chance in front of it. Thus, I conceived a plan that would ensure that Nanda would find no reason to make use of his arrow. I had to execute my plan and yet remain safe. My strategy was simple. It is an age-old strategy of looks that can deceive. I took on the most beautiful form that the earth had ever seen.

When I descended on the streets of Gokula, the menfolk became madly captivated by my beauty and began following me like a bunch of bees hovering around a flower. Praising my extraordinary elegance, they began to find fault with the beauty of the most beautiful damsels of the heavens like Urvashi, Rambha, and Menaka. They openly declared that my beauty was a million times more maddening than those celebrated *apsaras* from the heavens. My shy reactions to their comments excited them even more.

The women of Gokula were equally astounded. They began to whisper amongst themselves that this must surely be the goddess of fortune who had come to bless Gokula with her auspicious presence. I guess they concluded this because I was playfully twirling a lotus flower in my hand while walking on the streets of Gokula. Since the lotus flower is constantly in the hands of Lakshmi, the goddess of fortune, they concluded I was her. No one had even bothered to ask me who I really was and why I was in their village. They were too busy jumping to their own conclusions without bothering to find out the reality.

When they saw me walking towards Nanda Bhavan, they were actually saying that surely the goddess has come to bless the baby. The moment

I heard the word baby, my mouth began to water. I loved babies. Not in the way these humans do, but in my own special way. I have many babies in my belly. Sorry if it sounds too gross. This is a demon class joke so humans may not be able to appreciate it.

Though there were many babies in Gokula in the waiting, I was somehow drawn to Nanda Bhavan almost automatically. My feet were unknowingly pulled towards that house and I entered the courtyard of Nanda Bhavan. As soon as I stepped across the threshold, I realised that this wasn't an ordinary place. The vibes were so different. In fact, for the first time in my entire demoniac career, I was palpitating. I had never known what fear was, until that moment when an unknown and strange type of fearfulness originated in my heart.

Brushing aside the feeling, I stepped into the palace as if I belonged there, confidently putting on a brave front. No one even tried to stop me as I made my way into the bedroom where the baby was kept in a golden cradle. Totally ignoring his mother who was standing next to the cradle, I bent over to get a closer look at the baby. I didn't want her to feel any kind of concern or worry, which is why I focused on the child totally and tried to smile in the most loving manner that I could manage. From the corner of my eyes, I could see her melting in the thought that I had come to bless her child. I even heard her tell another beautiful lady there that if the child drinks my breast milk then surely he would become immortal as it was akin to drinking celestial ambrosia. She sincerely believed that I had come solely for that purpose. If only she knew what I was up to!

That very moment, the baby boy opened his eyes and stared at me. I thought I saw great anger flashing in them. There was something in those eyes that I had never seen in any other child so far. I was taken aback by the fierceness of his expression. But the very next moment, those eyes closed once again. I didn't know what to make of it and I wasn't even sure of what I saw.

Brushing aside those thoughts, I began to focus on the duty at hand. I carefully held the baby in my arms and expertly shifted him to one side and exposing my breast, I placed one poison-smeared nipple in his mouth. There it was! In the next moment, the baby should be lying lifeless in my arms. Usually, babies turn blackish-blue once they suckle me. But this baby was already blackish-blue even before I picked him up. Suddenly I felt an extremely painful stab in my breast. I looked down to see the baby latching on to my breast intensely and sucking with great force. It was a type of suction that was pulling out my very life-breath from within my body. The milk was long gone and so was the poison; now my life itself was being pulled out forcibly by that innocent-looking baby.

I began to scream in pain. The mothers were totally confused. A moment back I was peacefully feeding the baby and the next moment I was desperately trying to push him off my body. However, he wasn't interested in letting go of me. I even tried to forcibly push him away with all my strength and power. But he was latched onto me like a leech with his lips sucking away my very life. I yelled and screamed. Running out of the house like a mad woman, I went berserk on the streets of Gokula hollering out profanities. I couldn't retain my disguise. How can we be someone else when in pain? Who can act delicate and beautiful when about to die? I resumed my demonic form that was huge and horrible to look at. The villagers of Gokula, the very people who had admired me when I walked in my beautiful form, were now shrieking and running away from me in great fear.

Having reached the outskirts of the village and unable to deal with the pain anymore, I fell on my back with a heavy thud. The pain was increasingly becoming excruciating. Suddenly, I felt no more pain. In a moment, all the pain had vanished. I felt I was so lightweight, I was flying. The next moment I saw my own body lying lifeless below, on the forest floor. Crushed under it were numerous trees and plants. Playing on my body was that innocent little blue boy who was the cause of my death.

Though I was feeling bad about being expelled from my body so abruptly and so rudely, for the first time in my life I felt free and burden-less. I was at peace. There was no anger, there was no cruelty, and there was no fear. There was only a sense of peace and gratitude for this little child. This is what my father Bali had probably referred to as liberation. My body, which lay below, didn't matter to me anymore. It didn't matter that all the villagers who had gathered around, hacked my body and burnt it in a huge fire. It didn't matter that I didn't exist anymore. But two things mattered the most at this point. When my body burnt, everyone could smell an amazing fragrance. It was the smell of aguru. My demonic and absolutely impure body had become purified by the touch of that little child, who was now my Lord and Master.

The second thing that mattered to me was that I was immediately transported to another realm, which was way higher and way farther from this material world. It was the original spiritual world in the spiritual realm. But the most interesting thing was that my master gave me a position there that was so unique and wonderful. I was given the role of a nurse in the spiritual world. Though I came to destroy him, he only focused on the fact that I nursed him with my milk. Keeping that in mind and considering that to be my eternal desire, he granted me this role of his nurse mother in the spiritual world. Who could be kinder than my Lord!

CHAPTER 3

Sevika in Nanda Bhavan:

THE MAKING OF A BUTTER THIEF

f anyone is wondering how Kanha could be so naughty and steal butter at so many people's houses, I have the answer. I was the sole witness to how a one-and-a-half-year-old child became the celebrated butter thief that he is today. No doubt he was mischievous right from the day he was born. His naughty eyes said it all. But his real naughtiness began as soon as he got some movements in his limbs and was able to crawl and somehow stand on his own. The magnitude of his mischief only escalated as he grew in age. His fertile brain constantly thought of newer ways to be naughty.

I served as a maid at Nanda Bhavan right from the time Kanha was born. I have watched every phase of his growing up. I have seen him crawling around Nanda Bhavan enthralling everyone with his antics. He was sweetness overload. He loved everything colourful, especially Nanda Baba's turban. Whenever the colourful turban came within his reach, he grabbed it with both hands and pulled it out. As he grew into a toddler and could walk with a wobble, he would imitate his father's walking style. He would hold a stick and walk with it. While doing so, he would topple and fall. But, in spite of the struggle, he continued to imitate with great style.

Sometimes in great humility, he would carry the slippers of Nanda Baba on his head. At other times he would drag the heavy sword of Nanda Baba across the floor with great difficulty. When he was particularly naughty, he would stand on the edge of the well and peep into the depths almost causing a heart attack to mother Yashoda, who then yelled at the top of her voice and ran to save him. Kanha obviously enjoyed her reaction so much that he would beam from ear to ear.

One day he discovered his taste for butter. From the moment he ate it, it was almost like love at first bite. He loved it madly. That day itself he kept demanding more and more. He was almost insatiable. The next day he kept running around all over the house trying to find butter. That was when he made the greatest discovery of his life. He found the storeroom where the butter was stocked. His feet would automatically walk towards the store many times a day. But someone or the other would pull him away from there. His eyes longingly kept staring in that direction though he was physically pulled away from there.

Finally, he did what I always suspected he would do one day. It just happened much sooner than I expected. One afternoon while everyone was fast asleep, Kanha, who had feigned sleep, tiptoed towards the storeroom. I happened to be awake and saw him somehow wobble towards the storeroom, looking guiltily in all directions. From the fearful look on his face, I knew that he was heading for some mischief. I followed him quietly till the store. He looked all around to ensure no one was watching him. As soon as he was sure that it was absolutely safe, he stepped in. I peeped in just in time to see little Kanha make himself comfortable near a pot of butter. Then, he put his hand inside the pot of soft butter. He kept staring longingly inside the pot relishing the soft butter with his eyes first. Then he plunged his hand inside the butter pot gleefully. The look of excitement on his face was priceless.

He pulled out a handful of soft creamy white butter and held it to his mouth. Closing his eyes, he ran his tongue over the tasty butter. His eyes were closed for a long time, as he tasted the nectar dancing in his mouth. I could actually feel him relishing the love of mother Yashoda concealed in that hand-churned butter. Again and again, he kept eating the nectar from the butter pot. When he put his hand yet again into the pot, he was suddenly bewildered. The pot was missing and his hand was touching the floor. He opened his eyes in panic. He was shocked to see his mother standing right in front of him. She was looking at him sternly. She wanted an explanation for his behaviour. What was he doing in the storeroom in the middle of the afternoon when he should have been sleeping next to his mother?

For the first time, I could see that look of confusion on the face of Kanha, a look which is only visible on the face of a liar. He was obviously thinking quickly. He had to say the right thing or else he would get into great trouble. He knew his mother was very strict. He could easily fool his father but his mother was different. He began to stutter, "Mother . . . Mother, I . . . I . . ." Her penetrating gaze was too intense for him to handle. So, he lowered his eyes and continued, "The new bangles you had made me wear are too hot. My hands were burning so much that I had to put them inside butter to cool them else they would have burnt away like the cotton that burnt that day."

This was the most amusing reason Yashoda had ever heard from anyone till date. She almost burst out laughing but somehow managed to suppress her smile and spoke in a strict tone, "Show me your hand."

Kanha held out his hand and insisted that his hand was burning. Mother Yashoda carefully inspected his hand and realised that they were perfectly fine. He had fabricated a story to get out of this fix. She wanted to trap him in his own game. She remarked if that was the case then why was there butter around his mouth? Kanha had a quick answer to that too. He said, "There was an ant crawling on my hand. I kept trying to get it off but it just wouldn't budge. Finally, I had to wipe by hand against my mouth to take off the ant. When I did that, the ant did fall off but I didn't realise that a little butter may have rubbed off over my mouth. I didn't even taste the butter. I am not at all hungry now."

Yashoda was so amused by his quick-wittedness that she burst out laughing. Her anger just melted away in the puddle of his sweet innocence. His innocence simply gladdened her heart. She picked him up and carried him to the bedroom. I could visibly see little naughty Kanha heave a sigh of relief when his mother wasn't looking in his direction. He had indeed managed to squirm out of big trouble successfully. Along with relief, I could also see great confidence in his eyes. He had just managed to fool his mother. This was his first successful adventure as a butter thief. He was now sure that this could be his career option. While he was riding in his mother's arms, he had a triumphant look on his face. If he had managed to overpower his mother who, according to him, was the smartest *gopi* in Vrindavan, then fooling all the other gopis wasn't going to be difficult at all. Suddenly all the storerooms of Vrindavan seemed to be inviting him to plunder them. The historic adventures of the butter thief began from that day in Vrindavan. I considered myself fortunate to have been the sole witness to the first of them all.

CHAPTER 4

Nanda Baba:

HAPPY BIRTHDAY TO MY DARLING KANHA

Kanha's birthday is the sweetest and yet the toughest time for us in the family. We love it because it reminds us of our great fortune to have been chosen to be parents to such a darling boy. But we dread it because it also brings great pain to Kanha. To make myself clear, I need to share the story of every birthday of our darling son. His birthday always begins with elaborate pujas, rituals, prayers, fire sacrifices, and chants. The sacred rituals itself take a considerable amount of time. Organised by my wife Yashoda, these rituals have to be perfect and complete. She takes no chances when it comes to Kanha's birthday. She will do everything that Maharshi Shandilya recommends. This part is always the best and smoothest. No hurdles and no troubles. Kanha is always happy to be part of all the rituals and he loves to do exactly what the brahmans do, practically imitating them. Once the rituals are done, Maharshi Shandilya offers his blessings to Kanha and leaves along with his disciples.

As soon as the sage leaves, all of Kanha's friends surround him. Now it is their turn to enjoy Kanha's company. Just like the elder *gopas* and gopis bring various gifts, similarly, the small gopas also arrive with their gifts. But theirs are so very different from what the elders consider gifts. The elders bring jewels, expensive clothes, and unique toys. But the young friends of Kanha bring simple things that are sometimes too simple for adults to appreciate. Like this time, for Kanha's birthday, Bhadra gave him a very unique gift. He came to Kanha with a small box in his hand. He told my little son, "Kanhaiya, I will put tilak on your forehead. I have nothing to give but have got cow dung tilak that I want to decorate you with."

When Kanha heard this, he became very eager to have a tilak put on his forehead. He had seen me apply tilak on guests as a mark of respect. So, he felt very respected and happy when Bhadra offered to do that. He even wondered how Maharshi Shandilya could forget such an important part of the rituals. In fact, cow dung tilak should have been the first thing applied. According to Kanha, his friend Bhadra was so very clever to have thought of it. This was the best possible birthday gift anyone could have given him. As Bhadra applied the tilak, Kanha squealed in delight. The love of Bhadra was on his forehead now for everyone to see in the form of a beautiful cow dung tilak mark. Though Kanha was decorated from head to toe with beautiful ornaments and jewellery, he found the tilak put by Bhadra the most appealing and attractive. He ran to all the elders, showing off his special birthday gift from Bhadra. He kept saying, "See what my Bhadra has put for me."

All his friends offered him such innocent gifts. One small cute boy named Toke gave him a three-coloured flower. When Kanha received the precious flower, he jumped, hopped, and skipped showing everyone the new gift he received from Toke. His eyes gleamed with happiness. He repeatedly told everyone that no one had ever given him anything more precious than this three-coloured flower and that no jewel was as valuable as this special flower. Another friend presented him with a small peacock feather that looked so adorable. Yet another gave him a white lotus with five shades of colours. Some others got him flowers, fruits, leaves, or feathers. He was ecstatic about every gift that he received from his friends. He jumped and showed everyone those gifts as if they were rare gems. The elders had spent months collecting the best gift that they thought would excite Kanha. They spent a considerably large amount of wealth trying to get him the best of the best. But the excitement that Kanha showed in receiving simple gifts from his friends was impossible to match with his reaction to those expensive gifts.

Yashoda always decorated Kanha wonderfully for the occasion. Today his hair was draped with many strands of colourful pearls and a stone-studded crown rested on his head enhancing his beauty infinitely. She had instructed him to welcome and serve his friends by giving them return gifts. Since he had received so much joy from their presents, it was ideal if he could reciprocate by offering them special gifts. When he heard about this, I saw a sparkle in my little child's eyes. He was so thrilled about the idea. He ran towards a decorated table that was filled with gifts that we had accumulated throughout the year for this occasion.

This year we had collected the rarest of rare gifts from across the world to make Kanha happy while giving them away to his friends. Kanha was always particular about what he would give his friends and therefore it took us months to collect these gifts knowing how fussy he was in his choices of giving. But this year too, as it happened every year, this part of the birthday celebration turned out to be the most painful. Though the gifts accumulated by us were superlative and the best compared to all the previous years, still Kanha did not like them at all. We were stunned. Kanha did not find any of the things worthy of his friends. He looked at each wrapped up gift and felt disappointed. Compared to the fruit, flower, or leaf that he received from his friends, all these gifts appeared rather inferior. He compared the most precious gift on that decorated table with the tilak that Bhadra had put on his forehead and it appeared totally insignificant and pale. He threw away everything on that table and began to cry. He felt that he had nothing worth giving his friends.

Just a few moments earlier our little Kanha was jumping and frolicking around showing off the gifts that his friends had given him and now he was sulking at not being able to reciprocate sufficiently. In his frustration, he turned towards his brother and looked at him with big tear-laden eyes. Somehow, I have noticed that Balaram always finds a solution to his little brother's complicated problems. He asked

Kanha a very simple question, which was also a clue to the solution. He asked, "Kanha, think what is it that you have that will satisfy your friends and make them the happiest." Kanha began to ponder seriously over this deep query. He put his head down and thought seriously. Suddenly he found the answer!

He instantly knew what he had that made his friends the happiest. He jumped over the gems, clothes, and all the other gifts that he had thrown on the floor and ran towards Bhadra. Throwing himself into the arms of his friend, he began to shout loudly, "Bhadra, I am yours!"

When he said that, I observed his body language. He wasn't able to speak much but every cell of his body spoke volumes. With every cell of his body, Kanha had offered himself to his friend as a return gift. What could he offer that was greater than himself? What gift would be greater than offering oneself completely to one's friend as a gift? Kanha had gifted himself to his friend. For Bhadra, there could be no greater or more valuable a gift than Kanha himself. Nothing else was worthy or even remotely valuable in comparison. Kanha ran to each of his friends and gave each one a tight hug, screaming with every fibre of his being, "I am yours! I am yours!"

Toke, Sridhama, Varuthapa, Subal, all of Kanha's friends got an unforgettable return gift that day. This was my little Kanha's way of reciprocating with his friends and those he loves dearly. He left his friends forever in the debt of his love. They knew that no other friend, not even their parents, could love them as unconditionally as Kanha did. That's my Kanha for you. With a heart overflowing with love for everyone he calls his own.

CHAPTER 5

Pillar of Nanda Bhavan:

WATCHING KRISHNA'S NEW LILA EVERY DAY

Oh, my god! Kanhaiya was such a joker! He knew how to get out of sticky situations with his ability to joke. Not only was he a jokester, but also a name-caller. He had a name for everyone. Not one name but several names for the same person. He made them up on the spot. And there was no logic behind any name. He would give names to cows, bulls, calves, monkeys, birds, and even birds like crows. Because he was so small, he could not remember all the names he gave. Thus, he ended up giving the same person different names daily. Just yesterday, he had called a boy Ujjwal; and today he called the same boy Subodh. But he would purposely give the weirdest names to the gopis and especially to those who troubled him a lot. If anyone irritated him then he got back at them by giving them a weird name.

The most interesting part was why Kanhaiya got angry with the gopis. More often than not, it was his own wrongdoing. Imagine you go to someone's house uninvited and eat all the goodies and not just that, you break all the empty pots. Would that not make the owner angry? But, according to Kanhaiya's philosophy, no one was allowed to get angry with him, no matter what he did. Period! If someone did, then he would call them names.

Now you must be wondering who I am and how I knew all this. Well, there's nothing I didn't know because I was a mute spectator of everything that happened in the courtyard of Nanda Bhavan, which was the beehive of all activities.

I was the proud pillar of the courtyard and not a day passed when I didn't hear about the naughty lilas of Kanha. Every day the gopis gathered here and discussed about their Gopal. Every day Kanha's friends gathered here and discussed about their Kanhaiya. Every day the elders gathered here and discussed about their *lalla*. I was privy to every secret and everyone's desires. I was most fortunate to be here. In Vrindavan, everything had a consciousness, a mind, and thinking power. What I lacked was only mobility. But that was also of no use for me because Kanha himself spent his day here with me. Sometimes the children ran around me, sometimes they climbed atop me. Sometimes they hid behind me. I was their silent friend. What more could I ask for? Oh yes, there's one thing I didn't like and it was cats and monkeys climbing over me and scratching me. Very bad manners on their part, I must say. Someone needed to teach them etiquette.

Shhh! Wait a minute, the gopis were talking about Gopal again, and I wanted to hear what they were saying.

"Just today he ransacked a house. Not only did he and his friends eat all the butter and milk products there, but they broke all the pots, creating a total ruckus at her home. The gopi had gone to the Yamuna river to fetch water and by the time she returned, a royal mess was staring at her. The little brats did not leave a single pot intact. Highly irritated and frustrated, the gopi is on her way to meet Yashoda and complain about the little boy's antics."

"Yashoda!"

Sure enough, a gopi barged in yelling.

But even before she could say anything, she began to laugh hysterically. She was in a very agitated frame of mind, determined to even the score with the brat Kanhaiya, but the scene in front of her caused her to burst into peals of laughter. She completely forgot what she had come for. She laughed and laughed uncontrollably. She laughed till her stomach hurt. The cause of her laughter was hiding behind mother Yashoda.

Knowing well that this gopi would reach his house to complain to his mother, little Kanhaiya had strategically hidden behind his mother. When the gopi entered Nanda Bhavan, she was facing mother Yashoda. But because Kanhaiya was hiding behind his mother, she was also facing him.

Even before she could open her mouth to complain, Kanhaiya began to make funny faces. The three-year-old brat was making so many faces that the gopi could not help but dissolve into mirth. When he saw his trick working, he escalated his act. He opened his mouth wide like a monkey and showed his teeth as if to scare her. One by one, he continually made all kinds of funny faces— spreading his lips, showing his teeth, blowing up his cheeks, elongating his mouth, drawing his cheeks inside, puckering his lips, squinting his eyes, opening his eyes wide or closing them shut or rotating his eyeballs rapidly or making his eyeballs disappear completely. Sometimes twisting his face from one side to another. Every face and expression was the ultimate.

When the gopi saw all his amusing faces and dancing eyes, she couldn't hold on to her serious demeanour. She fell on the ground, rolling with laughter. The more she looked at him, the more hysterical she became, unable to stop laughing at his antics. Innocent Yashoda was totally unaware of the performance going on behind her back. She was wondering what had gotten into this gopi who came in storming in anger but suddenly was on a laughing spree. She kept asking her why she was laughing so much. But Kanhaiya did not allow her to catch her breath. He kept his comedy show on for a long time.

Finally, managing to get a hold on herself, she told mother Yashoda, "First look at your monkey behind you." Before she could say anything else, the laughter spree took over once again as Kanhaiya had once again escalated the tempo of his mimics.

Reaching behind her, Yashoda pulled Kanhaiya forward, holding his delicate little hand. As soon as Kanhaiya stepped ahead, his face assumed the innocent little-boy look. Gone were all the naughtiness and the continual weird faces that he had been making a moment ago. He could be mistaken for the most obedient and innocent boy in the universe. By now, all his friends, the co-conspirators in the rampage, had also arrived. Their bodies, hands, legs, faces, and even bellies were covered with traces of milk and curd, though they had tried their best to remove them. But that wasn't the context of this discussion at all now. Neither the gopi nor mother Yashoda even noticed it.

Once Kanhaiya was facing his mother he said, "Mother, she is Batanga!"

Mother Yashoda began to laugh when she heard the word. Batanga! This was the first time she was hearing it. She understood it was one of those made-up words of little Kanhaiya. She asked him, "What is Batanga?"

By then Kanhaiya had escaped from his mother's grasp and ran towards me. With his anklet bells tinkling, he hid behind me and said, "Batanga is the aunt of Matanga!"

Now both Yashoda and the gopi were laughing hard. Who was going to tell them who Matanga was? But Kanhaiya had made his escape by running out to join his friends, while Yashoda and the gopi laughed non-stop. She no longer wanted to complain. Kanhaiya's innocent nonsense name-calling had saved the boys yet again. And I had witnessed yet another lila of the great *liladhari* Sri Krishna, which no one else had seen.

CHAPTER 6

Yashoda:
THAT UNFORGETTABLE DAY
OF DIWALI

My life revolves around my little blue boy. From the day he was born to me, each day is a festival. Just admiring his buttery soft limbs and his beautiful smiling face is in itself a celebration. Oh, how I love my darling baby! Not just I, the whole of Vrindavan loves him dearly. Their love is so intense that I am left with no choice but to share him with them.

However, the happiest time for me is the night because I get to cuddle him all by myself. No one to disturb us and no one to share my little cutie-pie with. Festivals are busy days for me, as I need to prepare special sweets for my darling boy.

On Diwali day, I reluctantly pushed myself up to rise early, way before sunrise. The moment I moved, my little baby grabbed my clothes. He understood in his sleep that his mother was about to leave the bed. I almost melted into his arms once again. His sleeping form resembled a blue lotus curled up into itself. His navel was the golden whorl that the blue lotus was trying to hide from the world. Whilst my heart was giving up, my intelligence wasn't. The sense of duty and responsibility kept me from melting into the pot of love. I had to wake up and make sweets for my baby boy who would get hungry very soon. Diwali sweets took time, especially when made with great love.

I had been working on these sweets since yesterday. Whatever I made for my baby Kanha was always the best. I never compromised on the quality of the ingredients and the effort I put in. Though I had an army of maids eager to assist me in every chore, when it came to cooking for Kanha, I preferred to do everything myself. Our cowshed is home to nine lakhs of beautiful cows from which I had carefully selected eight of the best for the quality of their milk. I would offer these eight fortunate cows a very special type of grass known as Padma Gandha grass. This grass had the fragrance of lotus flowers and the cows eating this grass had milk with the sweet flavour of the lotus in their udders. I fed the milk of seven of these cows to the eighth cow so that her milk was the best of all. The result was unbelievably sweet. Her milk was thick and very fragrant. Every milk-sweet and milk preparation I made for my Kanha was from the milk of that particular superlative cow.

As I walked into the kitchen that Diwali morning, I had many pots of milk to deal with. Some of them were milk and some had been converted into yogurt that needed to be churned into butter. I wanted to finish most of the chores before my darling woke up because I knew very well that he would demand my complete attention. As I began setting things in order before beginning the cooking, the maids came rushing in to assist me in every little chore they possibly could. While I allowed them to handle all the peripheral tasks, I chose to focus on the main preparations.

Keeping a huge pot of milk to boil, I sat down next to a grinding mortar and began churning. I have recently observed that there is some kind of sync between my mind, lips, and my hands. As soon as I begin using my hands in trying to serve Kanha, my mind begins to think about his playful activities and my lips begin to hum a song about it. I prefer to remember everything my baby does in the form of beautiful songs. As I was singing and churning, a sort of musical concert began in my kitchen. The swishing sounds of the rod dipped in yogurt that I was churning combined with the tinkling of my swinging earrings and jingling bangles created the musical beats that enhanced my singing.

Suddenly everything froze! My churning abruptly stopped. My eyes were closed while I was immersed in the memories triggered by my song. When the churning rod came to an abrupt halt, I opened my eyes to behold the most beautiful sight in creation. My little darling was standing next to the grinding mortar tightly holding the churning rod in one hand, stopping its movement. Placing his other hand on his hips, he was showing his unhappiness at my abandoning him in his sleep. That sight of my Kanha melted my heart as time stopped for me. I smiled at him while he frowned at me, feigning anger. His eyes seemed to be speaking to me. They were telling me to stop this churning business and feed him. My little Kanha was hungry. I have observed that he is hungry every time he sees me. That was his way of showing his love for me. Dropping the silken rope that held the churning rod, I held out my open arms. My little baby jumped into my arms immediately, forgetting his anger.

As I placed my Kanha on my lap and began feeding him milk, there was a look of contentment on his face and a beautiful smile radiating all over his face. He closed his eyes and relished my liquid love. As I was gazing at his beautiful face, a sudden smell caught my attention. It was unmistakably the smell of milk boiling over. Immediately I put Kanha on the ground and ran over to the stove to save the pot of precious milk that I had so painstakingly collected to make sweets for him. As I reached the pot and picked up the boiling milk, it seemed as if the milk was staring at me in great anger for having offered so much of my milk to Kanha. The milk in the pot seemed to be upset that it's not going to be able to serve my baby today. Maybe I was thinking too much. Everything in Vrindavan seemed to have a life of its own from the moment Kanha was born. I even imagined trees bending themselves to touch Kanha when he crawled past them. Anyway, I had averted a big catastrophe by making it on time to save the milk from boiling over. Now we would be able to prepare sweets in the right quantities as planned.

Just then I realised that in the heat of the moment, I had dropped Kanha on the ground while he was drinking milk. My baby must be so upset with me. *Let me go back and take care of him, the rest can wait,* I thought. I got the biggest shock of my life when I reached the churning area. The place was a royal mess! The churning urn was broken and liquid yogurt and churned butter were flowing out, forming a puddle at its base. Emerging out of that puddle was a pair of tiny footprints. It took me no time to figure out what had transpired in my absence. But I was surprised to note that the naughty Kanha was intelligent enough to understand that if he struck the pot at its bottom it would not create a noise that would alert me inside the kitchen. As I was about to follow the little footsteps, I noticed the door of the storeroom swinging. I walked in to find a much greater mess in there. Kanha had broken all the pots of butter, ghee, milk, and yogurt that were stored there. Not just broken them, he had taken pains to splatter all the ingredients on all the walls and the floor. He had left no stone unturned to pass on the message that he was highly upset for being neglected like that.

By now, the sun had already risen and our house had become a beehive of activity with scores of people moving about in all directions, minding their own duties and services. Though I had so many things to do myself, I had to first stop the notorious mischief monger who was on the prowl. Asking the other gopis to take charge of the kitchen, I followed the trail left by Kanha. The trail led me outside the kitchen area towards the courtyard. On my way out, my eyes spotted a thick bejewelled stick my husband often used on his walks. I picked it up knowing very well that sometimes a mother has to be strict and teach her naughty child discipline. Though I hated this part of parenting, I had to do it for the well-being of my child.

When I reached the middle of the courtyard, I was stunned at the scene in front of me. Kanha was seated dangerously on a wooden grinding mortar. I had no idea how the little fellow climbed so high. But what was even more shocking was that there was a group of chattering monkeys with sharp nails and sharper teeth sitting very close to him around the mortar. The naughty boy had a pot of butter that he had just stolen from the store and was distributing the contents to these restless monkeys. I had spent so many hours making such good butter and here he was, throwing it away to monkeys. This was the naughtiest and the most dangerous thing I had ever seen him do. I couldn't contain myself anymore. I ran towards the group of monkeys with the stick raised high in the air menacingly. The monkeys began to run helter-skelter as soon as they got a glimpse of the stick. My son, who had by now become an un-proclaimed leader of the monkey gang, dropped the butter pot, jumped off the mortar and sped away from me. I couldn't believe that he actually managed to jump such a distance and still retain his balance though he did wobble a wee bit initially. Surely my son was growing up rapidly. But all those thoughts were for later. For now, I needed to catch the prankster and teach him a good lesson on discipline.

Although I ran behind him as fast as I could, Kanha ran much faster. He ran as fast as his little legs could carry him and I was running as fast as my heavy body would allow me to. Being the mother of an energetic child wasn't easy. Whenever he turned back to look at me, I could see great fear in his eyes. He was already crying in fear and his eyes kept shifting between my face and the raised stick that was terrorising him. For a moment I thought that I should drop the stick if it was scaring my child that much. But immediately I had another thought—that this was the time to discipline him for that unacceptable behaviour.

By now, the flowers in my hair were falling apart and toppling to the ground. My dress was loosening due to the heavy chase I was on. My legs were faltering in exhaustion. When I felt I couldn't keep up any longer, I put in one last effort and managed to catch my fleeing child. When I caught him, he became hysterical and began to wail loudly looking at that stick. With trembling lips, his eyes were shedding copious streams of tears. When I saw the state of my child, I threw away that stick immediately. Though I wanted to discipline him, I didn't want to traumatise him. I immediately pulled him into my embrace. Kanha was sobbing uncontrollably now. The black mascara on his eyes had melted away flowing down his cheeks like two black rivers. I realised that this boy was too disturbed to be left alone. Though I wanted to be with him and console him, I had to rush back to attend to my duties in the kitchen. Moreover, he had created such a mess that it had to be cleaned before insects and flies began hovering.

With so many things to do at once, I realised that there was only one solution. I had to keep my disturbed child out of trouble and yet be peaceful enough to engage in my own duties without having to worry about his mischief-making. As I was looking for a solution, my eyes darted to the wooden grinding mortar that Kanha had sat on just a few moments before. I concluded that the partner in crime has to become a partner in punishment also. Pulling my son to the wooden grinding mortar, I made him stand right in front of it, with his back against it. Kanha had quietened a bit by now. I wasn't so angry and the stick wasn't in my hand, so there was no reason for fear. But he was clueless about what I was up to. He looked at me, confusion writ all over his face. I asked one of my assistants to get me a rope.

Placing the rope around the mortar, I pulled the two sides around Kanha's body and tried to tie a knot. I realised that the rope was a little too short. I asked the maid to get another rope to tie with the previous rope. She got one and soon I realised even then the rope was a bit too short to tie Kanha to the mortar. More ropes were brought and still the combined length of all ropes fell short by almost two fingers distance. The gopis ran to the cowshed and got all the ropes that held thousands of cows. Still, the sum of ropes fell short by exactly two fingers. I couldn't fathom the miracle. Whatever it was, I was determined to tie Kanha to prevent him from getting into more trouble.

No matter how many ropes came in, the distance was exactly two fingers short. Soon the whole of Vrindavan got involved in the rope festival. From every house, ropes came in the dozens. I kept tying them together to hold Kanha and it was still exactly the same distance short. Without my perception, time flew. It was already evening and I had been trying to tie ropes all day, literally from sunrise. I was exhausted and drenched with perspiration when a drop of it fell on Kanha's face. My plan of tying Kanha wasn't going to happen now. Perhaps, Lord Narayana did not want me to punish my child. I almost gave up my plan, but my hands which were so used to tying knots all day, out of habit tied another knot. And surprisingly that was the final knot that bound Kanha to the wooden grinding mortar. The gopis clapped and began to shout out, "Damodar!

Damodar! Damodar!" Kanha had earned himself a new name, Damodar, which meant one tied at the belly.

Exhausted but happy that it had finally happened, I got up and walked into the kitchen to handle the duties that were abandoned from the morning. I cast a glance at my little boy who was so longingly looking in my direction from where he was tied up. Though I felt sorry for him, I pulled myself away from the sight and rushed into the kitchen. An hour passed. I got so completely involved in the cooking and cleaning that I lost track of my little boy. Suddenly I heard a massive sound that sounded like the strike of a thunderbolt. It was so loud and coming from such close quarters that it startled all of us. We ran out of the kitchen towards the courtyard. The first thing I looked for was my Kanha. He was missing!

I panicked. Running like a maniac, I reached the outside of Nanda Bhavan where a great crowd had already gathered. Pushing myself through the crowd, I reached the middle of the assembly. What I saw shocked me greatly. Two massive Arjuna trees that had always stood outside the courtyard of Nanda

Bhavan had fallen down, causing that tumultuous sound. The worst thing was that between the two fallen trees was embedded the wooden grinding mortar to which Kanha had been tied. I had no idea how the mortar had reached there and I had no idea where my darling baby was. Everyone seemed dazed and too shocked to react. My husband Nanda had arrived and someone had already told him about the story of me tying up Kanha to the mortar. He was glaring at me angrily. I was already dying of guilt and now my husband was upset with me. More than anything else, Kanha was still missing.

"He's here!" Suddenly we heard a villager shout out in joy. Those words brought out a collective sigh of relief. Everyone jumped up and reached little Kanha who was well hidden within the foliage of the two huge trees that had fallen. Around him were a few of his young gopa friends who were least bothered that everyone around was worried. They seemed to have invented some new game that they were animatedly talking about. When Kanha saw that I had come, he simply ignored me and looked in the direction of his father. I was so hurt when he did that. I was simply trying to protect him but inadvertently I had ended up putting him in life-threatening danger. Nanda Maharaj untied Kanha and picked him up in his arms. The father and son walked away talking animatedly. I could see that Kanha was complaining about me while coolly ignoring me.

I rushed into Nanda Bhavan drowning in the sorrow of being disconnected from my son who had purposely avoided me. Diwali had turned into a major disaster. Like Ramachandra had been reunited with his mother, I was hoping that someone would help me reunite with my son. For a long time, the father-son duo was missing. My friend Rohini managed to pull me up and engage me in preparing a meal for the family. While I was busy, the pain of separation did not haunt me as much. But the moment I heard Kanha run into the house with his father tagging behind, my heart ran out to him. But he once again ignored me. Sitting in his father's lap, he ate food lovingly from his father's hands. The tension between the mother and son was too obvious in the dining room. My husband, who was an expert in dealings and the art of mediation, did something very unique to reunite us.

After the meal was over, he raised his voice and expressed his desire to punish the culprit who had tied Kanha to the grinding mortar. He declared that as the king of Vrindavan, he had the authority to do that and he would spare no one even if the culprit was his own wife. When Kanha heard that I was going to be hit with a rod for my mistake, he immediately jumped up and ran to me with his arms flanking me protectively. He began to shout hysterically that no one should touch his mother. No one should punish her. He embraced me and began to cry, trying to save me from Nanda Maharaj's wrath. Immediately Nanda Maharaj softened and smiled. Mother and son had been reunited once again. Diwali was complete with the reunion of yet another mother and son. All's well that ends well.

CHAPTER 7

Balaram:
BUTTERFLY ATTACK!

The rainy season had just got over and the weather was pleasant in Vrindavan. This was my favourite time of the year when Vrindavan is lush and green. We got to play all we wanted all over Vrindavan on the soft grass. But on this day, we had a funny encounter. Not just funny but very funny.

When the weather was so good outside, who wanted to remain inside the house locked up? I pulled Kanhaiya, my darling brother, and ran towards the door. Our mothers had already dressed us nicely. I was wearing my favourite blue dress and Kanhaiya was wearing his favourite yellow dress. Our mothers had put beautiful turbans on our heads too. Though the turban was heavy, they told us that we looked like small kings wearing them. Parents have a different sense of dressing. When we entered the forest, we changed the dressing to our style, which meant forest flowers, leaves, and fruits. Who liked these gold and diamond necklaces and bracelets? Anyway, that is for later; let me tell you what happened in the morning as soon as we opened the doors of our house.

We were many boys rushing out together at that time. Bhadra was there, Sridama was there, Subala was there, and so were many more. We were so happy to get to play so early in the day. Jumping, dancing, and talking animatedly, our excited group reached the door of the house. We pushed it open. And then it happened. A butterfly happened!

An orange-coloured butterfly came fluttering in through the open doorway. We were fascinated by its colour. As we stared at it with wide-open eyes, it circulated us and chose to land on my head. I froze! In my three years of existence, never had any insect sat on me. I didn't know what to do now. But Kanhaiya got really angry. He was saying, "How dare this lowly butterfly sit on my *Dau's* head? My brother is a king! How dare this insect sit on the king's turban?" I was now more amused by his anger than at the butterfly. As I was wondering how to manage the butterfly on my head, Kanhaiya began to wave his fingers over my head with great speed trying to shoo away the butterfly that had made my turban its destination.

With all the hand movements, the butterfly took off from my head. All our friends became excited at Kanhaiya's success. He had moved the arrogant butterfly. Everyone began to clap and celebrate his achievement. Kanhaiya felt proud and was all smiles. Suddenly his smile faded and a look of panic set in on his beautiful face. He screamed out loud. This was totally unexpected! The orange butterfly that had flown off my turban had now landed on Kanhaiya's finger. Initially, the butterfly was moving on the finger . . . probably adjusting itself into a cosy position. Then it settled down and stopped moving completely. Just like the butterfly had frozen on his finger, Kanhaiya had frozen onto the floor. He wasn't moving an inch. Only his eyes and eyebrows were moving and his mouth was screaming. He was desperately trying to tell us to save him from that butterfly. We began to laugh loudly at his plight. He looked so cute in panic mode.

And why would I shoo the butterfly off from Kanhaiya's hand? I could never shoo anyone away from Kanhaiya. I loved to bring everyone close to him. But seeing his desperate situation, all of us did our best to help little Kanhaiya. We waved our hands, jumping up and down, running all over, screaming and yelling. But nothing worked. The butterfly was stuck permanently on Kanhaiya's finger!

Kanhaiya was scared to even move his finger, not wanting to harm the delicate creature. But he was more scared for his finger. What if the butterfly ate it up? I was thinking that once someone takes shelter with Kanhaiya, why would they even think of leaving? I was almost sure that the butterfly would never ever fly away, just like all of his friends who never wanted to leave his company.

But what happened next was even more unbelievable. From out of nowhere, thousands of butterflies came fluttering into our house through the doorway. They were of all colours, sizes, ages, wing patterns, and shapes. They began to circumambulate us as we panicked and screamed at the top of our voices as if attacked by dangerous demons. Kanhaiya was frozen with just one butterfly but now with thousands of them around, he was totally hysterical and joined in our screaming spree. Soon all those butterflies perched themselves on us. They sat on any part of our bodies that caught their fancy. Shoulders, arms, heads, bellies, backs, everywhere! In moments, all of us were covered by a blanket of hundreds of butterflies of various colours. Could it be that our bright turbans, bright clothing, and small sizes had given them the impression that we were all small flowers full of nectar? Kanhaiya surely was. Everyone in Vrindavan loved him so much, so he must surely be very sweet to taste.

For the butterflies, it was festival time. Our screams only managed to move them from one limb of our body to another. And some moved from one boy to another. By now, the butterflies had become quite bold and fearless. We were in big trouble. We were in a very sticky situation. We could no longer help each other now. We needed external help—of adults. We began to shout for our mothers to rescue us. My mother Rohini and Kanhaiya's mother Yashoda came running, hearing our calls. They were stunned at the sight they saw. All our bodies were covered completely by beautiful and colourful butterflies. The mothers tried their best, waving their hands, shooing away the butterflies. But the butterflies had become so stubborn that they sat on them too. Now what would we all do?

CHAPTER 8

Sevak in Nanda Bhavan:

KANHA IS CRAZY ABOUT COWS

Being a servant in the house of Nanda Maharaj and Yashoda Rani was a divine experience. I have lost count of the number of years that I have been serving here in this palace. I am very much an integral part of their family now. Of all the things I liked to do in Nanda Bhavan, the one that I looked forward to the most was serving snacks in the evening after the boys got back from their cow-grazing task. Though that meal was so unpredictable in terms of the number of boys coming to eat, it was the sweetest exchange of the day. Yashoda always assumed a higher number and prepared special dishes accordingly. Little Kanha brought in so many of his friends to eat with him. These friends of his never wanted to let him out of their sight so they happily followed him home when invited, although they had been with him all day. Something very special happened today evening during their snack time.

The boys had just returned from the forest and bathed. They had all changed into comfortable clothes. A few other boys who had gone home to bathe had also joined them here at Nanda Bhavan. I began handing out dishes of rice dipped in sweet milk, which was one of Kanha's favourite meals after the forest expedition. While they were eating their food, the boys animatedly discussed their day's happenings and other things that they had just been told by their mothers. Anything the boys heard or experienced, they would immediately want to share it with Kanha.

The funniest and the cutest was a little boy named Toke. He always had something funny or interesting to say though he was so small. Today he had information that caught the attention of everyone there. With milk dripping down his chin, Toke whispered in Kanha's ears secretly, "Pavitra is going to give birth."

Kanha's eyes became big on hearing that. He immediately stopped eating and turned towards Toke and asked, "How do you know?" This news amazed Kanha because Toke was much younger than him and was, in fact, the youngest amongst all friends. How did he get to know something that none of the others knew? Seeing Kanha's amazement, Toke felt oh-so-proud. He boasted that his mother told him.

In fact, he added another point to prove his point further. "That is why she was not sent for grazing today."

Now it all made sense to Kanha since he had been wondering all morning why Pavitra had not come along with the other cows to graze. Kanha remembered every cow and every friend personally. Even if one were missing, his day wouldn't feel complete. I was now in the dining area with some bowls of steaming rice dipped in the best milk of Vrindavan. The set of boys that were seated with Kanha that day was always there every day. Toke and Bhadra never left Kanha's side practically all day. After their bath, the boys looked so charming and fresh. With no decoration and ornaments on his body, Kanha looked so much sweeter. Mother Yashoda always felt that as soon as the boys came from the forest, they need to be bathed and fed sumptuously with tasty refreshments. And it was my duty to ensure that they all ate enough.

Try as I might, the boys would never sit in a line or in any sort of disciplined way that would make serving or monitoring their quantities easy. They were too restless to even sit in one place. Within the span of that one meal, they would have moved at least ten times. Today they were not moving but rather huddled together discussing an important secret that, apparently, they didn't want to share with the adults. A few drops of golden milk were glistening on the abdomen of Kanha. The other boys too had milk spilt all over their bodies. While I was admiring the beauty of the scene in front of my eyes, Kanha turned to me all of a sudden and asked a question. "When will Pavitra give birth?"

The question was so sudden and unexpected that it shook me out of my meditation and I replied without thinking of the consequences. I said, "She has just delivered. The calf is as white as milk." As soon as I said that, I realised my mistake. But it was too late now. All the boys immediately stood up with a squeal of surprise. They ran out leaving behind their half-finished bowls. After receiving that wonderful news, they couldn't wait a moment more. They simply had to see the newborn calf before it was too late. It was the most important event in their lives.

As soon as mother Yashoda and Rohini saw the boys running out without finishing their meal, they ran after them trying to stop them. But the boys had no time to even wash their hands and mouth. The angry mothers glared at me for spilling the beans on the new calf's birth while the children were eating. I could obviously do nothing but hang my head low. I had indeed made a grave mistake. I should have revealed the news only after they had finished eating. Out of a sense of responsibility, I volunteered to fetch them back. But Yashoda realised that getting them back in this excited state was next to impossible. Best was to arrange for a meal there itself. So, I set out to do exactly that.

By the time I reached the cowshed where Pavitra had given birth to the baby calf, Toke's mother had already fed all of them forcefully. While the kids were marvelling at the newborn calf, she had managed to make them eat. Pavitra's calf was as white as her mother. The newborn wasn't even able to stand as it was born just a few minutes ago. The children watched in admiration as they saw the mother licking her baby. As soon as Kanha stepped in closer, Pavitra mooed loudly and turned her face towards him. She began to smell Kanha but knew well enough not to lick him with her tongue. She had probably guessed that the boys had just had a bath. Several times she stuck her tongue out to lick but turned her head away just in time. From the moment Kanha had entered her shed, Pavitra had almost forgotten her own baby. But Kanha pushed her head towards her baby and said, "You lick baby!"

Both Kanha and Balaram together turned her face towards the newly born calf. Pavitra obeyed and began to lick her calf once again. But after a few moments, she helplessly turned her face towards Kanha and began to smell him once again. Now the calf tried to stand up. Kanha saw the struggle and helped the baby stand and began to encourage her lovingly. "Stand up! Get up! We are there with you."

The calf somehow managed to stand and began to smell Kanha. Suddenly her legs wobbled and she fell down. Kanha helped her stand once again, held her face and kissed it. The calf finally managed to stand on her own and sniffed Kanha again. She had forgotten her mother and had eyes only for Kanha. Perhaps this was the first thing that the calf learnt from her mother. To keep looking at Kanha and keep smelling Kanha. As I stood there looking at Kanha lovingly dealing with that calf, I was thinking how fortunate that calf was to learn to stand with the help of Kanha. When Kanha helped, how could anyone not stand?

CHAPTER 9

Rishabh:
MY ADORABLE FRIEND AND DOCTOR, KANHAIYA

We had the best doctor in Vrindavan. He was a doctor like no other. Everyone had complete faith in him and he loved to treat everyone even if they didn't actually need treatment. In fact, his name itself was medicine. I heard from so many big-bearded sages who came to Vrindavan that this is what all scriptures say. But for us little boys, we didn't need any proof of scripture. We believed in his healing touch. Kanhaiya was our little doctor.

There was no one in Vrindavan who didn't want to be touched by this doctor or be in touch with him. Everyone's happy experience was that Kanhaiya's touch took away all pain. If anyone in Vrindavan experienced any pain, they would want the magical touch of the little prince of Vrindavan. They would go to him and say, "O Kanhaiya, there is pain in my head. Can you press it a little?" My friend Kanhaiya could never say no. In fact, he would be eager to relieve his kith and kin from any kind of pain. He would drop whatever he was doing, even if he was playing his favourite game, and turn his attention to the person who sought his help. He would make them sit and then press their head with his tiny fingers.

During this process, he was always very serious. His countenance showed he was in the middle of a very important job. He felt responsible for their healing. How could he heal if he wasn't serious about it? But since he was so small, how long could he press? No one wanted to trouble him or tire him. As soon as he started pressing their head, that patient would hold his hands and say, "Enough Kanhaiya. As soon as you touched my head, my pain ran away." Kanhaiya was so small and innocent that he would look here and there trying to see if he could see the pain running away. He thought pain was a bird or a cat that he could see. That innocent moment was a sight worth seeing.

All my friends have made him their doctor. While playing and frolicking in the forests of Vrindavan, many of us would get hurt from the thorns and the rough bushes. Just today my arm had a mild scratch. It was so mild that I didn't even notice it. But somehow our doctor friend always noticed these scratches no matter how small. And anytime he saw even a minute scratch, he immediately got into medical action. He pulled my arm carefully to inspect the scratch. He began to ask me serious questions. "Rishabh, how did you get that ugly scratch? Tell me so that I can heal you quickly."

The funny thing was that the scratch was so small that even I couldn't see it. I kept asking him where it was. I even told him it was nothing and tried pulling away so that I could go back to play. But Kanhaiya had already gotten into his doctor role by then. He was quite serious. "No Rishabh! Don't touch it. If not treated immediately, these scratches become infected and get septic. It will become more painful if I don't heal it now itself."

Kanhaiya was a very sensitive doctor. If anyone had the slightest wound, whether it was a friend or a cow or a bull or a deer or even a monkey, Kanhaiya would notice it. Even if an animal had a slight limp while walking, Kanhaiya would notice it. Kanhaiya did not miss seeing anything. He was always alert and caring. As soon as he saw it, he slipped into his healing mode at once. The best part was his treatment. His treatment was always unique. He would make a juice of whatever leaf, flower, or fruit that he found nearby. If he couldn't find those, he would go for any grass or even mud. Basically, whatever he could lay his hands on was good enough for his healing purpose. This healer was not bothered about any specific species of grass or flower or fruit or leaf! He could turn anything and everything into healing medicine.

So today while trying to treat my scratch, he plucked some leaves from a plant nearby and with great care he began to crush them with a stone turning them into a pulp. He then held my arm with both his hands and bent down to blow carefully on the scratch. He blew air several times from his mouth and gently stroked his fingers over it several times. Then he said, "Now it's time to apply the medicine over your wound." With great care, he applied the pulp on my scratch. It seemed as if he was curing some major incurable disease. I couldn't control my laughter because I wasn't feeling any pain at all and the scratch hardly even existed. I could have easily gone to play or even taken care of the cows. But I knew that if I laughed or ran away, Kanhaiya would feel hurt, even insulted—and sulk. I never wanted to see tears in his big eyes. So, I felt it was best to allow him to continue his treatment.

Once he applied the medicine, he asked, "Rishabh, is your pain any less now?"

I couldn't stop my laughter anymore and said, "But I didn't have any pain."

He ignored me and continued his enquiry, "Now can you tell where the scratch was?"

Because there was so much juice all over my hand, the scratch was not visible. Finally, Kanhaiya was satisfied that the scratch had gone. "It has healed!" he declared happily.

I was touched by his concern. Was there any other doctor who attended to sick people with so much care? If a doctor attends to you with so much love, how can any scratch or any disease remain uncured?

CHAPTER 10

Parrot in Vrindavan:

EAVESDROPPING ON KANHA
AND HIS FRIENDS

hese boys are so hilarious. The kind of conversations they have are so serious and at the same time so amusing. If someone had to listen to bits and pieces of their conversation, it would seem like two senior citizens speaking but when you hear them in totality, they are overflowing with humour. I was sharing this with a group of my parrot friends.

I am Daksha, leader of the parrots and also Sri Krishna's pet parrot. I have access to some of the most confidential pastimes of my master. Today I was fortunate enough to hear the most hilarious conversation that took place in the forests of Vrindavan, when the boys took their cows there to graze. My parrot friends were all ears when it came to stories connected to Sri Krishna.

Some of the boys are too young to understand everything and yet they say complicated things with so much confidence. Just yesterday I heard Tejasvi speak in great fury. He was holding Sri Balaram's hand and urging him to action. Little Tejasvi was saying, "Dau, get up and pick up your stick. It's time to kill all the demons and their uncle also."

It was hilarious to hear that little Tejasvi thought that Kamsa was the uncle of the demons. He was too young to understand relationships. He had no idea whose uncle Kamsa was—whether he was the uncle of the demons or of Sri Balaram. But one thing he understood: that Kamsa was a villain because he kept sending demons to Gokula all the time and caused so much trouble to the villagers. Tejasvi had been disturbed for the last two days particularly because both days the demons came exactly when he was about to win a game they were playing. He wasn't scared of the demons but he preferred them to plan their visit and not disturb his game. So, when Tejasvi burst out, Sri Balaram diverted his mind by beginning a new game.

Today, once again a demon attacked and this time Devaprastha was very angry. He and Tejasvi came running to Sri Balaram. They wanted to confront him and find a permanent solution to this nuisance by the demons. I could see that Sri Balaram was tired of answering the questions of these little boys. He feigned sleep. The other boys had scattered in small groups and were sitting all over the place. Some of the bigger boys like Arjuna, Vishal, and

Varuthapa had gone to bring back the cows that had wandered farther away. When Devaprastha and Tejasvi saw that Sri Balaram's eyes were closed and he seemed to be in deep sleep, they were confused. Looking around, the little innocent boys found Sri Krishna sitting under a Kadamba tree with his legs stretched out on the lush green grass. His hands were resting on the ground and his head was arched behind and he was reclining against the tree. On one side on the grassy surface was his flute and on the other side was his cow-herding stick.

The two little boys walked up to Sri Krishna and sat down close to him. Sri Krishna loved these two little kids. Devaprastha was a charming boy who didn't seem to be from this world. Everyone loved him and affectionately called him Dev. Touching Sri Krishna's arm, Dev asked seriously, "Kanhaiya, where do these demons live?"

Sri Krishna had a surprised look on his face. He immediately caught hold of Dev's hands. Pulling him closer he asked, "Dev, why are you asking this question? Are you scared of them?" Dev came even closer to Sri Krishna and said, "Why should I be scared?" By this time Dev's eyes were big and animated. He continued his version of what the demons were. "I know for sure that these demons are weak. They may look big and scary. They may scream a lot but they are actually soft like balloons. That is why you are able to beat them up so easily."

Sri Krishna began to laugh at that innocent definition of a demon. To continue the fun, Sri Krishna probed further. Putting his hands behind his head and resting on them, he asked, "Then why do you want to know where they live? Will you go to their house if you know where they live?" Sri Krishna was enjoying teasing the little boy.

Dev burst out energetically. "Oh yes! We both should go there and catch as many demons as possible and bring them back with us." What a fertile imagination! Sri Krishna was amused by this idea.

He asked Dev what he would do with the demons. He wanted to know the logic behind why this little boy wanted to catch demons and bring them back to Vrindavan. Dev had his reply ready. He said, "We will use the demons to scare the gopis!"

He was so happy with his own idea that he began to clap his hands in joy. He continued, "If the demons jump or shout too much, we will just poke their tummies and they will burst *phuttttt.*"

Sri Krishna laughed loudly at the idea and then decided to teach the little boy something important. He said, "Demons cannot be tamed like pets. They are disgusting and very, very dangerous. If you do not kill them as soon as you see them, they will bite you. So, we cannot bring them with us here. Anyway, by now Uncle Kamsa has very few demons left with him."

Dev immediately had a follow-up question based on Sri Krishna's answer. If demons could not be tamed then how did Uncle Kamsa manage to tame them? Sri Krishna explained to little Dev that Kamsa himself was a demon. I could see mixed emotions in Sri Krishna when he was speaking about Kamsa. There was so much anger and hatred in his voice. This was a big secret revealed to Dev. He was surprised to know that Uncle Kamsa was also a demon. That led him to ask another question, "If Uncle Kamsa is also a demon then why do the big gopas speak highly about Kamsa? Why are they scared of him?"

Sri Krishna smiled at the boy's inquisitiveness.

He replied that the big gopas are simple people and they don't know that demons are weak. Sri Krishna explained that when they hear the scream of the demons and look at their huge sizes, they get scared. That seemed to make sense to little Dev because he had seen that whenever demons came, the big gopas and gopis began to run calling out to each other in great fear. They shut their doors and trembled in fear. But the children were not scared at all. Because the children knew the reality of these demons. They had seen Sri Krishna kill these demons with a flick of his hand. He didn't even have to exert himself. And the most important thing was that Sri Krishna was one of the weakest of the boys. Once even Dev had defeated him in wrestling. Dev felt that though Sri Krishna may be older than him, he was definitely weaker than him.

Dev had one final question for Sri Krishna that day. He asked him, "Is the king of the demons Kamsa as fat and as scary as the other demons?"

Sri Krishna again spoke in great anger. Whenever he heard Kamsa's name, anger filled his heart. He said, "I have not seen him yet. But the day I see him, I will kill him."

The parrots listening to my story trembled as they could almost experience the fury of Sri Krishna through my words. These words of Sri Krishna became prophetic. Dev by now was scared of Sri Krishna's angry mood. He embraced him and said, "No, no! You don't go anywhere near the demons and the demon king."

Dev didn't say it out loud but he was now apprehensive. What if the demons bit his weak Kanhaiya? Demons were so bad!

CHAPTER 11

Bhadra:

MY ADVENTURE WITH THE BUTTER THIEF

It was fun to be with the butter thief when he was on the prowl. He had such unique ways of stealing butter from the gopis. Never did he repeat a trick. Every siege would be exceptional and fun. I am proud to say that I, Bhadra, his best friend, have been on many such missions with Kanhaiya. Of all the fun-filled adventures we have had, one simply stands out as the most fun-filled.

It was early in the morning when Kanhaiya knocked on the door of a gopi that fun day. After careful deliberation, we usually selected the target the previous evening itself. We chose this gopi's house based on feedback from one boy who had recently been to her house for a meal with his family. His mouth-watering experience eating the soft butter there immediately became our reference point. Kanhaiya had a new idea for looting this house. He straightaway went and knocked on the door of the gopi's house. We all panicked and ran away to hide. We had no idea what he was up to.

The gopi who opened the door was pleasantly surprised to see Kanhaiya standing at her doorstep.

With a broad smile, she asked him, "O Kanha, what are you doing here so early in the morning?" I can imagine the pleasure of the gopi seeing the darling of Vrindavan first thing in the morning, a sight that any resident of Vrindavan would consider most fortunate at the beginning of the day. Usually, people would have to make some lame excuse to go to Nanda Bhavan to see Kanhaiya first thing in the morning. But today he himself was standing in front of her house. With his cute little smile, he looked so adorable. If only she knew the sinister motive behind that smile!

Kanhaiya yawned. His hair was dishevelled and his eyes had a sleepy look. He was trying to show the gopi that he had just woken up from his sleep and had been sent to her house right away on an important errand. He said in a sweet, sleepy voice, "Mother Yashoda sent me. There is a very big sage coming to our house today and we have run out of butter. She wanted to know if you could lend us some. She promised to return it as soon as possible. Since it's too late for her to make fresh butter, she felt that the butter made at your house could be the best alternative. She loves the quality of the butter you make."

The gopi was very happy to hear the praise about her butter and that too from mother Yashoda who made the best butter in Vrindavan. To convince her even further, Kanhaiya added that she would in fact receive two pots of butter in return for her one pot. The gopi needed no further convincing. She was already excited just by hearing his words and exclaimed, "O' Kanha, no need to return the butter. I am just happy to send the butter with you. Mother Yashoda asking is itself so rare. Please tell her that the butter that I am giving you is my service to the sages. I do not expect anything in return."

The gopi ran in and returned with two pots of butter filled to the brim. In addition to the two pots of butter, she also gave Kanha a packet of crystal sugar. She said that the combination of butter with crystal sugar would be perfect. A big smile appeared on Kanha's face along with a naughty look. What more could an innocent boy ask for than this lip-smacking butter filled with crystal sugar!

Once Kanha held the pots in his hands, the gopi bid him farewell and closed the door. As soon as he heard the sound of the latch, Kanhaiya signalled to all of us to come out of our hiding places. We were at his side in a moment with our eyes literally bulging at the sight of the two pots of yummy butter. We looked at Kanhaiya with pride and love. This boy was a genius. How smartly he had outwitted the gopi to part with her precious butter and, that too, voluntarily!

But Kanhaiya did something that totally surprised us. He settled down right there at her doorstep with the two pots of butter. We were flabbergasted. We kept telling him that it was unsafe to sit there. If the gopi opened the door, we would be finished. But Kanhaiya was adamant. His logic was that it would be great fun to eat the stolen butter at the doorstep of the house from which we had stolen it. He said that if we ate elsewhere, the excitement wouldn't be as much as the danger of eating it at the doorstep of the gopi.

Of course, we loved his idea! He always came up with such far-out strategies to have fun. We settled around him on the steps of the house while he began to distribute the soft butter to all of us. He then dropped sugar crystals over the butter in our palms. The combination was heavenly. As we munched, enjoying the yummy delight, we completely forgot the world around us and delved deeply into the buttery delight swirling in our mouths. The crystals crunched between our teeth, the butter touched every inch of our palates and our tongues danced savouring the sheer ecstasy.

Suddenly, the door opened! The gopi stood there, staring furiously at us with fiery eyes that looked as though they were about to burn us down. What we hadn't realised was that while we were enjoying our meal, the sound from our biting of those sugar crystals was very audible even from inside the house. The gopi was surprised to hear so much noise coming from the door. She thought that it was a group of chattering monkeys that were creating a nuisance. Little did she imagine that she was in for a major shock when she opened the door and found us sitting there devouring her butter. She was shocked beyond imagination and so were we, to see her standing there.

She began to yell at Kanhaiya, "You mischievous boy! Didn't you tell me that the butter was needed for the sages who were visiting your house? Why are you eating it here? Don't you have any shame? Your poor mother must be waiting for the butter."

She was really irritated at Kanhaiya for duping

her like this. She had just lost her precious handmade butter. Kanhaiya stood up and spoke with great power, "Gopi, please mind your language. Don't you know that these friends of mine are no less than sages? Look at them carefully."

Most of us were confused about what to do as we had chunks of butter in our hand but were unable to eat them. Our mouths and faces were smeared all over with butter. It dripped from our hands onto our stomach and thighs. Our eyes were open wide in shock. This was the range of sages that the gopi was looking at. Kanhaiya continued his dialogue, "Look at this one. This is a *naga* sage who travels around the world without any clothes."

Kanhaiya was pointing to one small boy in our group who wasn't wearing any clothes. In fact, that boy was so young that he didn't even realise that we were caught and he was still licking his palms, wiping off all the butter. The gopi was furious at Kanhaiya for conning her so shrewdly and her chest heaved in great anger and frustration. He went on to say, "You should do *dandavat* obeisance to these sages who have so kindly come to your house and accepted your offering."

The gopi retorted, "Yes, let me offer my dandavat obeisance to these sages by getting my *danda* (stick) and beating them up. Tell them not to leave, just wait here until I return."

As the gopi ran in to get the stick, we realised that it was time to wrap up. We ran away as fast as we could, abandoning the butter pots right at the doorway and leaving the place in a complete mess for the gopi to clean up. What a fun day it was! Now I am eagerly waiting for my next adventure with the butter thief! One more house to be looted, more butter to be eaten, and more bliss to drown in!

CHAPTER 12

Himalayan Bird:

MY SAVIOUR, MY MASTER, SRI KRISHNA

was born in the Himalayan jungles. I belong to a unique species that is not found in other parts of the world. Hardly anyone has seen me outside the Himalayan jungles. Only a rare few dare to step into the icy expanses of the Himalayan jungles and therefore our species remained unknown for a long time. Until one day, when a hunter entered our jungles and caught poor me.

As I fell into his trap and he laid his hands on me, I could see the sparkle in his eyes. He had never seen a bird with such fascinating colours. After caging me, he danced and shouted out rather wildly, declaring that I was more beautiful than a peacock. I had lost my freedom and he had gained a source of income. He taught me various tricks and I learnt everything faster than he expected. That made him even more possessive of me. I picked up a few human words and that delighted the hunter even more. He stopped hunting and focused on taking me around to various villages and earning an income through bird shows.

One fine day, my life went through a complete transformation when we stepped into the land of

Vrindavan. A crowd of beautiful young boys and girls gathered around us. It looked like a festival day as the whole village had gathered together for some event, all dressed in brightly coloured clothes. The hunter was delighted to see the crowd. He enthusiastically began to flaunt me around. With great pride, he declared that I was an auspicious bird and everything I spoke came true. He announced that I hailed from the snow-clad Himalayan mountain ranges and a bird of my colour and capability was not just rare but almost impossible to see.

As soon as he made those statements, I spread my wings and hovered over his head, showing off my variegated colours to the spellbound kids. Their jaws dropped in amazement. They had never seen anything more fascinating. Even the peacock seemed pale in front of me. They were not just fascinated by the colours on my body but were enthralled by the fact that I could speak their language. The hunter declared that the kids could ask any question and the bird would answer them.

There was a buzz after that announcement and the kids were animatedly discussing with each other. Suddenly, from the height that I was seated,

I saw the most beautiful scene I had ever witnessed. A beautiful young child who had a blackish-blue complexion came running out of a palace. He was so beautiful to behold that I almost forgot to flap my wings for a moment. I was stunned by the charm of that little child. He wove his way through the crowd and jumped onto the lap of an elderly person who seemed to be the head of that village. I later learned that the elderly person was Nanda Maharaj, the king of Vrindavan. That little boy was Sri Krishna, my eternal master. I still remember the first time I saw my master. It was love at first sight. As soon as he saw me, he immediately wanted me and as soon as I saw him, I wanted to be with him. When he jumped onto the lap of his father, the first question he asked his father was, "Why is that bird tied with a string?"

While everyone else focused on my colours and speaking abilities, Sri Krishna was interested in my freedom. There was a fine black almost-transparent thread tied to my leg and the hunter held the other end of that thread. I could fly to a certain extent, enough to show my wings to the onlookers but not enough to escape. When Sri Krishna asked that question, my eyes brimmed with tears. No one had shown so much sensitivity towards me. I kept my eyes and ears on him as he sat on his father's lap, flanked by his brother Balaram on one side and his best friend Bhadra on the other side, both of them casually leaning on Nanda Maharaj.

The hunter kept urging the kids to ask me questions. A little boy named Devaprastha walked up to Sri Krishna and said, "He must be in pain. Poor bird is tied up." In response, Sri Krishna turned to his father and began to lovingly stroke his beard. He said, "I want this bird, Baba." Even before Nanda Maharaj could respond to his son's request, his brother Balaram spoke. He said, "Please give your bird to our prince. You can claim your price."

The hunter was thrilled. He wanted to strike the best bargain possible and become rich pronto by cracking a good sale. He kept telling them about how he got me from the Himalayan snow-clad peaks. But deep inside, the hunter was in a dilemma; maybe selling me was not such a good idea. I had ensured a recurring income for him for the first time in his life. Selling me would end that and fetch a one-time income. In this confusion, he was making contradicting remarks that discouraged the sale. He said, "Since the bird is from the cold Himalayan ranges, it may not survive here."

I realised that this was my chance to save myself from the clutches of the cruel hunter and be in the divine company of the compassionate Sri Krishna. I quipped, "I won't die here. I will live for a long time. Please let me live here."

The hunter was shocked at my open expression of intent. Now he had no choice but to let go of me. He had to undo his statement. He said, "This bird is all-knowing. If it says that it can survive here, then surely it can. The prince can have it."

As soon as the hunter agreed, Sri Krishna jumped out of his father's lap with great joy and ran towards me. At the same time, the hunter released the thread and I hurried to perch myself on the little fingers of Sri Krishna, my eternal master. The hunter gave the thread to Sri Krishna, who held it gently. Nanda Maharaj ordered for a huge basket of jewels to be delivered to the hunter. The man was shocked by the amount of wealth offered in exchange for me, a mere parrot. He wasn't aware that in Vrindavan, bringing Sri Krishna a moment of pleasure was priceless—no amount of wealth could match it. This wealth was enough to ensure that many generations of this hunter's family thrived and prospered without having to work. With eyes wide with joy, the hunter embraced his fortune. No one left Vrindavan empty-handed.

When handing me over, the hunter warned Sri Krishna not to let go of the thread as I would fly away. But I immediately intervened and said, "I will not fly. Whether you keep me tied or untied, I will not fly away. I have been tied for a long time now. Until now, being tied made me sad. But to be tied to you will only make me happy."

Sri Krishna placed me on the finger of Balaram and began to untie me. All the young boys gathered around to watch. Sri Krishna does not like to see anyone in bondage. After untying me, he lovingly asked me if I would eat roti or flatbread. The hunter immediately quipped that the bird only ate fruits. I interrupted and declared that I would eat anything that is offered to me lovingly. In fact, I told the hunter to shut his mouth and leave as I now belonged to Sri Krishna and to the land of Vrindavan. Saying this, I proudly sat on Sri Krishna's right shoulder. Little

Toke came running with a piece of roti to feed me and I happily nibbled the roti.

Sri Krishna and his friends were so happy in my company. He told me lovingly that his mother would get me a golden cage to live in. He declared that the cage would protect me at night. During the day, I could travel with them to the forest and nibble on the hundreds of varieties of sweet fruits available there and fly as high as I wanted. Suddenly, little Krishna asked me a question. He wanted to know if I would give birth to a child. I was pleasantly surprised at his innocent question. I told him that my wife could lay eggs but that she was very far away in the Himalayas. Sri Krishna immediately declared that I should go and bring her to Vrindavan. He promised me that he would feed her too with roti and fruits. But I was scared to venture anywhere away from Sri Krishna now. What if some other cruel hunter caught me and tied me up? Sri Krishna reassured me that I was now his responsibility and so was my family. Upon my master's urging, I spread my wings and flew overhead circling Balaram, Toke, Bhadra, and Sri Krishna. I kept circling them as I went higher and higher. Sri Krishna kept looking at me till I became completely invisible. He loved me and I loved him.

CHAPTER 13

Rohini:
DEFEATED BY THE EXPERT LOGICIAN

urely there was some past connection between Kanha and the monkeys in Vrindavan. Either he was running behind them or they were running behind him. I had told him so many times not to gather them together like that. He just wouldn't listen. These days he has become a big logician. I have no answers to some of his questions. Just the other day I had a long discussion with him and he thoroughly defeated me with his logic.

It all began early one morning, when I saw him sitting amidst a group of monkeys in the courtyard of Nanda Bhavan. I ran up to him and asked him why he kept gathering the monkeys. I have noticed how, with one signal of his, a large number of monkeys entered the courtyard boldly. I was afraid that his association with them was making him restless like them. Association does matter, right? Of late, he had started showing many signs of restlessness in his behaviour. One day I saw him pick up a baby monkey. Another day I saw him climb on the shoulder of a big fat monkey. Though I knew that the monkeys loved him, they were animals, after all.

What could be expected of them? What if Kanha fell and hurt himself?

If he was concerned about feeding them, I assured him that I would keep food outside the courtyard for them. There was no need to call the monkeys inside. But did he listen? No! As soon as I turned away, he called them back inside. The worst thing was that this group of monkeys did not like to go anywhere else. It seemed as though they had been friends with Kanha for quite some time now. From early in the morning they jumped around on the walls of Nanda Bhavan as if waiting for a signal from Kanha. They stayed close to him all the time. If he left Nanda Bhavan and went elsewhere, not a single monkey would be on the premises. They followed him like his shadow.

I had also observed that if I kept food for them, they refused to touch it. Only when Kanha offered something, they immediately jumped at it. Even if Kanha and his friends pulled their tails or ears, the monkeys preferred to stay with them. Seeing their camaraderie, I once asked Kanha if he was a *vanara bandhu* or friend of monkeys. He nodded enthusiastically and said, "Yes, yes!" He immediately accepted the title as if it was the highest honour one could receive. I told him that it was not good for him. He immediately wanted to know why. When I told him that the monkeys were not good but he was good, he immediately got off from my lap as if offended and began an argument, defending them. He kept repeating that they were very good creatures. The rest of the monkeys in the world may be bad but the ones that come to Nanda Bhavan every day were good.

I argued that they jumped around and were a nuisance. He immediately replied that his mother also called him *chanchala* or restless and that she blamed him for being a nuisance. When he said this, mother Yashoda was nearby and glared at him. He looked away and kept his gaze on me. I wanted to continue the sweet discussion. Talking with the talkative Kanha was fun. I told him that the monkeys were looters and they snatched things all the time. Moreover, they were also dirty. Kanha asked me a bouncer of a question. He asked me if they were animals. When asking me this question, he lovingly held my face with his hands and looked into my eyes. I replied that because they were animals, they were not good, not realising that I willingly fell into his trap of logic.

With a smile, he replied that our cows and bulls were also animals. They are also so dirty because they pass urine and stool anywhere. Logically, he concluded that they were also not good going by my logic, due to the same disqualifications as the monkeys. They were also restless and they too passed urine and stool everywhere and that made them dirty, too. Based on this he asked me if I believed them also to be bad. Now how could any gopi in Vrindavan consider cows to be bad? I was in a spot and had to defend myself. I reasoned that cows are worshipped like God because they are *rishabha* dharma. I made up some jargon to win the argument. But he quickly said that monkeys are also God. I argued with him that if they were God, would God snatch other's things? I loved this discussion. He was so clever.

Little Kanha had an answer to that too. He asked me if the monkeys did farming or cattle-rearing or any other business. I replied negatively with a smile. Where was he heading? But he continued by saying that they also got hungry and they also needed food to survive. I argued saying that it did not mean that they should rob and snatch others' food as they liked.

He gave an explanation that stumped me totally. He said that the monkeys were different from humans because they did not think of food as yours and mine. For them food was food. They didn't believe in storing and saving like humans. They ate what they got immediately and didn't think about the future. Whatever they got, they directly put in their mouths. Because they think food is food, they didn't think too much about snatching or finding. If no one gave them food or if they didn't find food naturally, they snatched it. What was the harm in snatching for survival?

I was totally dumbstruck at his ability to argue with so much logic at this age. I turned towards Yashoda, who was laughing uncontrollably, holding her stomach. I told her that her son has become a logician. She laughed and said, "Rohini, maybe our son has learnt logic from the monkeys."

My perspective of looking at the monkeys changed from that day. I no longer considered them a nuisance. Everyone had the right to survive.

I began to look at them with more empathy and Kanha's relationship with them with more interest. But I always wondered . . . where did he learn so much logic?

CHAPTER 14

Gopi:
GOVINDA'S NON-STOP HARASSMENT

Govinda was our life and soul. But he was also so difficult sometimes. He troubled us a lot. He always picked up quarrels with us. What I didn't understand was that if he liked us then why did he trouble us so much? Not that we didn't trouble him. When he tried to play his pranks on us, we got back at him with the same intensity. There were some places in Vrindavan that were his "naughtiness" hideouts. When he wanted to play his tricks, Govinda did great research. He knew well in advance when and where he could find his target and at what time.

One day, we—the younger gopis—were crossing the narrow path of the Govardhan hill carrying pots laden with the best of butter, milk, and yogurt from Vrindavan. Just as we reached a spot that was so narrow that we just couldn't turn without spilling all our goods, we spotted Govinda's friends. This meant nothing short of a disaster. We knew that Govinda was somewhere around. Suddenly we could hear cracking sounds that echoed in the valley. Sure enough, it was the sound of our pots cracking. Someone was stoning us. More stones came continually and more pots broke. By the time we realised what was happening, we were totally drenched in milk, butter, and yogurt leaking from all the pots. Our clothes were fully drenched and soiled. Our hair was sticky with the combined fluids. We were naturally furious when we saw Govinda emerge from his hideout from where he was pelting us with all those stones. His friends had simply served as a distraction to keep our attention away from where he was hiding and planning his ambush.

He was deliriously happy to see us dishevelled and in disarray. It was a matter of pride and success for him because his tricks had worked. He could see the look of exasperation in all our eyes, especially Radha who was most furious. The way he laughed and mocked us made us even more determined to seek revenge. We decided then and there that we would strike back soon. He had also obviously expected that, but little did he realise that we would strike back the very next day. We knew that he and his friends would come to play the same trick on us the next day as well. But we had reached the venue much earlier and scattered, hiding, waiting. When Govinda came with his friends, he looked around with no inkling of what was in store for him. He began to show off to his friends, recollecting his achievement of the previous day. He kept boasting about the messy state we were in after he shot down all our pots. His words only rekindled our memories of distress and fired us up even more to seek revenge.

We waited patiently for all the boys to gather there and at Radha's signal, we jumped out of our hiding places. Govinda and his friends were totally bewildered seeing us springing out of nowhere and ganging up against them. They were just six or seven of them but we outnumbered them in hundreds. A huge mismatch in numbers. The boys escaped hastily leaving Govinda alone in our trap. Or rather, should I say we allowed all the boys to escape, so we could focus all our energy on Govinda. He knew his game was over. Checkmated. He had no choice but to obey us. He turned around completely and became totally submissive, begging for forgiveness with great humility. We knew very well that hidden under that humility was a big trickster and that we shouldn't fall for his innocent begging. Suddenly Lalitha brought out something that shocked Govinda. It was the dress of a gopi. Govinda immediately knew what was going to happen.

Holding him tightly we dressed him up as a gopi, just like us, but with a twist. We put the kurta (top garment) below and the skirt, above. He looked so hilarious. And embarrassed too. We were having so much fun at his cost. All our anger dissipated in the melting pot of his embarrassed discomfort. Now we teased him to get the maximum mileage out of the situation. Govinda shrank shyly in the midst of so many of us, that too dressed so awkwardly. We then made him hold a pot of milk on his head. Then, some of us threw stones and broke the pot at several places. In moments, he was fully drenched in milk. We did not stop at that. Next, we put a pot of yogurt on his head and then broke that too. Next, with a pot of butter. Soon Govinda was in the exact situation we were in the previous day. Our revenge was complete now and our anger had subsided. Tit for tat, deserved the brat! While we walked back happily to our houses, unknown to us, Govinda's mind was racing again, busy planning to get back at us, seeking revenge on revenge.

The next day, we were on the errand of transporting many pots of butter to the other side of Mansi Ganga. It was a huge lake and extended practically from one end of Govardhan to the other end, breadthwise. When we reached the banks of the expansive lake, we realised that there was just one boat there. We had no clue where all the other boats had disappeared. Having no option left, we got into that one boat, somehow managing to squeeze in with all our pots. The boatman seemed very strange, fully covered by a large, thick blanket. Only his eyes were visible from the little gap across his face. He spoke in a very hoarse and scary voice. Though all of us shivered with fear at his voice, we stayed in the boat because we had no choice but to hire this boat with its bizarre boatman.

The boat slid out slowly onto the calm lake. An eerie silence followed as the boat glided towards the middle of the lake. Suddenly, strong winds began to blow. The atmosphere underwent a sudden transformation instantly. We couldn't understand how such a dramatic change could happen so quickly. Now the boat also began to rock heavily. We were terrified. The boatman wasn't even looking at us. Neither did he appear scared. These storms seemed to be a routine part of his life.

When the storm worsened, we had to approach him for help to deal with the rocking boat. He simply asked us if we knew how to swim. We answered in the negative. He said that the only way the boat could be saved from capsizing was if the load in the boat was lessened. He suggested that we throw some of the butter pots into the lake. Naturally, given the circumstances, the value of our lives was more important than the pots of butter, and we threw some of them into the lake to lighten the load.

As soon as we did that, the boat began to rock even more. He declared that we needed to throw all the pots into the water to save our lives. We desperately threw each and every pot into the lake. The water around us turned white, with so much milk, butter, and yogurt floating around. For some time, the boat seemed to stabilise and glide smoothly. In a short while, the rocking began once again. Again, the boatman said that the load had to be lessened even further. He suggested that we throw away all the heavy jewellery we were wearing to bring some stability to the boat. We did exactly that, no questions asked. Soon all of us were stripped of our ornaments. We had thrown everything, including our earrings and bangles, into the lake.

Once that was done, the clouds became dark all of a sudden. The boat began to rock heavily—yet again. Radha got up, walked up to the boatman, and began to scream at him in anger. He refused to even look at her, turning away from her to face the opposite direction. Radha suspected some foul play and went closer when lightning struck. The sound was so sudden, intense, and close that Radha lost her footing and fell on the boatman. As soon as this happened, her expression changed completely. Gone was the fear. Gone was the uncertainty. She managed to stand up and put her hands on her hips, looking indignant. We were shocked at her change of expression. She pulled the blanket off the boatman and threw it into the lake. And lo and behold! It was Govinda in place of the boatman!

All this while, Govinda had tricked us and literally taken us for a ride. The rocking boat, the lightning, the sudden thunderstorms, were all his shenanigans. He was capable of doing anything, especially when it came to taking revenge when insulted.

CHAPTER 15

Naga Patnis:

THE MAGICAL TRANSFORMATION OF
OUR HUSBAND, KALIYA

We had warned our husband so many times not to venture into Vrindavan! Yet he did not heed these warnings. Now look at the trouble he has landed himself into. But in the land of Vrindavan, even punishment was actually love. In the world of the *nagas* where we hailed from, there was no real love. Not even fake love. There was only envy and hatred. The venomous presence of our husband Kaliya in Vrindavan was like an incurable disease of the heart. The lake connected to the Yamuna river where we resided, and resembled a woman holding a ball of fire within her belly.

Every single day we saw Sri Krishna and Sri Balaram. Though they passed by the lake several times, they never ventured close to the water. We could see through Sri Balaram's smart strategy of carefully keeping the adventurous Sri Krishna and his friends away from the poison-filled lake. But today was a different day. We were excited to see the boys led by Sri Krishna, walking towards our lake. When we saw the young boy and the cows drawing closer, we were both happy and worried simultaneously. Happy that Sri Krishna, the master we worshipped, was coming to our abode. Worried that the poisonous watery grave created by our husband would kill all of them at once. What an irony it was! We wanted to serve and our husband wanted to destroy.

We noticed that Sri Balaram was not with them. We later came to know that it was his birthday and his mother Rohini had retained him for a special 'shanti bath' on the occasion. The weather was so warm that the boys were tempted towards the cool waters of the lake. Though Sri Krishna tried to stop them, their excitement took over and they rushed into the lake along with the cows to quench their thirst and cool their bodies. By the time Sri Krishna reached the banks of the lake, the inevitable had already happened. All the boys and the cows lay dead!

That one moment touched our hearts the most . . . when we saw tears running down the beautiful cheeks of Sri Krishna. How much he loved his friends and his cows! From our hiding place, though we could see everything and though our love for our master was swelling up, we did not have the guts to approach him now. How could we, knowing that the cause of his pain was due to our husband's misdeeds? We chose to wait and watch. We were greeted by the greatest miracle we ever witnessed. With just one glance, Sri Krishna revived all the boys and the cows from the death snarl. It appeared as if life-giving nectar just oozed from Sri Krishna's eyes. The boys were excited to see themselves alive again. They embraced their friend gratefully and declared that indeed Sri Krishna had given them *sanjivani rasa* to revive them once again.

Once his gang was safe, Sri Krishna turned his attention to the lake that had caused such unpardonable damage. He noticed that the soft waves of the lake connected to the Yamuna river had a crimson golden radiance, the effect of the fiery poison emanating from the nostrils of our husband Kaliya, the thousand-hooded snake king. Dense black smoke lingered over the lake, indicating the presence of a raging fire within her belly. The waters of the lake were literally boiling due to the heat of that poison. The lake that Kaliya had taken over was about eight miles wide, situated in the southern part of the Yamuna river. Deep within the lake, using the mystical science of *jala sthamba*, Kaliya had created a magnificent city with a spectacular palace of his own. Though we lived in the company of our children and followers happily within the comforts of that palace, the destruction that Kaliya's poison had caused to the environment and animals in the area was terrible. There were no fish left alive in that lake. No vegetation survived for a considerable distance around the lake. Even the birds that flew overhead dropped dead on inhaling the fumes rising from the lake.

We could see Sri Krishna staring into the lake with great anger. He seemed to have decided to put an end to all the atrocities of Kaliya for good. He cast a glance all around the lake to ascertain the situation and the damage caused to his Yamuna and his Vrindavan. Spotting a single tree that survived in spite of the prevailing dangerous and poisonous atmosphere, Sri Krishna walked up to that tree. It was the same Kadamba tree on which Garuda, our greatest enemy but also the greatest devotee of the Lord, had perched for a few minutes.

Legend has it that Garuda had perched on this tree while returning from the heavens after procuring the celestial nectar of immortality. Before handing over the pot of nectar to the nagas, Garuda had sat on this very tree sipping a few drops of that nectar from the pot. While the great Garuda was doing that, it seemed that a few drops of that nectar had spilled on this tree, immortalising it in history. Sri Krishna swiftly climbed onto the topmost branch of that tree. When we saw the Lord and Master standing there with his hands on his hips staring down at the lake, we were mesmerised by his beauty. Even in great anger, he appeared so attractive. Tightening his waist belt and his turban, clenching his fists, Sri Krishna readied himself for a big fight. In the past, from afar we have witnessed Sri Krishna kill many demons who came to trouble the residents of Vrindavan. But we had never seen him tighten his belt the way he did now. For most demons, he didn't need to think twice before vanquishing them. We realised that whenever he readied himself by tightening his belt, he considered it to be a serious fight. We trembled in fear when he did that before taking the plunge. He gave one look of reassurance to the boys as if telling them to stay outside and take care of the cows. He was going on a mission. Just as a kingfisher dives into a river to catch its prey, Sri Krishna jumped into the poisonous lake to find his arch enemy.

When Sri Krishna plunged into the lake, the deadly poison rose into a mass of foam creating a wave that splashed high. The boys and the cows on the banks of the lake retreated hurriedly at the sight of that massive wave rushing towards the banks. Though we have always heard that Sri Krishna was lighter than a feather when mother Yashoda carried him, today we realised that if he chose to, he could also be heavier than a mountain. The effect that the jump had produced outside the lake was nothing compared to the effect it produced inside the lake. The entire civilisation that Kaliya had created within that lake had been disturbed. The intruder's jump had agitated everything within that lake. None of the snakes could ignore the impact of that jump. It was obvious to the naga community inside that someone from outside was challenging their very existence. Kaliya rose from his watery abode to terminate the trespasser. Little did our husband realise that we were the trespassers in Sri Krishna's abode, Vrindavan.

Kaliya emerged from the lake with his thousand hoods poised in the attack mode. When he displayed his full majesty, Kaliya's form was astounding. The boys on the shore gasped seeing the grandeur of Kaliya. But Sri Krishna was least bothered. He swam around in a playful mood, not even looking in the direction of the massive snake behind him. With his thousands of bloodshot eyes, Kaliya glared at the beautiful form of Sri Krishna dressed in yellow silken garments, wearing a garland of Kadamba flowers around his neck, his body shining like a newly formed monsoon cloud, with a pleasant smile on his divine face, swimming around blissfully. While we were mesmerised by the beauty of our Lord and Master, Kaliya lunged ahead at a great pace, and coiled around Sri Krishna, biting him hard on his chest. How could he be so cruel, especially with someone who was so divinely beautiful? We realised that was the nature of envy. Envy prevents you from seeing beauty.

At the horrifying sight of their friend in the coils of this massive snake, all the boys on the banks of the lake collapsed one by one, unconscious. Vrindavan was so intimately connected with Sri Krishna that the moment Kaliya captured Sri Krishna in his coils, there was a mammoth transformation in the whole environment of Vrindavan. Jackals shrieked harshly. Smoke and dust spread in all directions, blanketing the sky. The sun appeared dull and lacklustre. Terrifying winds began to blow in all directions. Violent earthquakes shook the plates of the earth. The bodies of living beings all over Vrindavan began to shake. The men felt a trembling on their left side and the women felt it on their right side. In an instant, everyone's mind was filled with anxiety.

With no idea about what had happened, everyone came out of their houses and assembled on the streets. Their only immediate concern was Sri Krishna's well-being. They rushed towards the Kaliya lake. Though the lake itself was more than eight miles wide, the Vrajvasis had no problem in locating the exact whereabouts of Sri Krishna since they had a very simple tracking mechanism in Vrindavan. They simply followed the footprints of Sri Krishna, decorated with sixteen symbols. Though thousands of gopa boys and cows followed Sri Krishna when he ventured out into the forest, they were all careful not to step on those divine footprints. Thus, Nanda Maharaj, mother Yashoda, and thousands of Vrajvasis soon gathered around the lake in the middle of which their darling Sri Krishna lay trapped in the coils of that humungous serpent.

When they saw the fearful scene, they broke down. Many fainted, shocked at the sight of Sri Krishna trapped by the poisonous snake. Mother Yashoda was hysterical at the plight of her little child. Nanda Maharaj, though equally disturbed, was putting his energy into holding Yashoda and restraining her from rushing into the poisonous lake. Though every single person in that assembly was disturbed beyond comprehension, the only one who stood there smiling was Sri Balaram. We immediately realised the reason behind that smile. After all, he was the original snake Seshanaag. If anyone could understand the importance behind that smile, it was us, the nagas. Sri Balaram was the original spiritual master of the universe and the all-knowing personality. He smiled knowing very well that Sri Krishna could never be trapped by anyone unless he chose to be. Sri Balaram knew that his brother was waiting patiently within the coils of that insignificant water snake for a reason. And the reason was a grand one. Sri Krishna was waiting in the coils simply to ensure that every single person in Vrindavan had gathered around to witness the greatest show on earth, which he was about to perform. While Kaliya was busy feeling proud of trapping his enemy in his coils, Sri Krishna was busy planning his performance.

Suddenly Sri Krishna expanded himself and the grip of Kaliya tightened around his body. The very next moment, Sri Krishna shrank himself to his regular size and thus the grip of Kaliya loosened, giving him the space to make his escape. In the next moment, Sri Krishna swam to a safe distance away from the thousand-headed serpent. Kaliya was furious at losing hold of his prey. He lunged forward to recapture Sri Krishna, but the Lord slipped away effortlessly. He was swimming around, playfully dodging the heavy-bodied snake. Sri Krishna was so flexible and agile that Kaliya couldn't trap him no matter how hard he tried.

Sri Krishna kept circling around until Kaliya was tired just by the crazy chase. His head was spinning and we could see a dazed look in our husband's eyes. Before he could regain his stability, Sri Krishna did something unbelievable. Forcefully bending one of his heads, Sri Krishna put one foot on the shoulder of Kaliya and climbed his way up to his head. As soon as Sri Krishna stood on the head of the massive serpent, conch shells blasted from all directions heralding his victory. Soon the conch shells were accompanied by sounds of *dundhubis*, kettledrums, and hand cymbals. All the unconscious men, women, and boys were awakened by the tumultuous sounds. As the Vrajvasis pushed themselves up from the ground, they were amazed by the scene that greeted them.

Standing on top of the tallest head of Kaliya was Sri Krishna in his classic three-fold bending style with one hand holding the flute on his lips and the other hand holding the lashing tail of Kaliya. When Sri Krishna saw that he had the attention of every single Vrajvasi there, he began his transcendental dance.

Seeing the Lord dance, the *gandharvas*, *siddhas*, *charanas*, and *apsaras* from the heavenly realms assembled in the skyways. With great pleasure they began to accompany the Lord's dancing and expert flute-playing with their drums and other instruments. As Sri Krishna danced gracefully on the heads of Kaliya, the demigods rained flowers on his transcendental body. Sri Krishna used the hundred-and-one most prominent heads of Kaliya as his primary dance floor. And what a dance floor it was! It was slippery, it was constantly mobile, it was lighted by diamonds that sparkled on every hood of the snake. Though it was the most challenging of dance floors, Sri Krishna moved with an elegance and grace that put the most expert dancers to shame. He was the original fine artist demonstrating to the world a form of dance that was never ever seen before.

Everyone was amazed at the grace with which he danced. He would time his jumps in a way that was in synchrony with the movement of Kaliya's various heads. Though the heads were all moving in various directions and in an uncoordinated way, Sri Krishna seemed to know which head would rise next. Every time Kaliya raised a head, Sri Krishna landed his feet there and smashed it down. The feet of the Lord are soft like petals of lotus flowers. But when those very feet landed on one of Kaliya's heads, they appeared harder than a thunderbolt. Every time Sri Krishna's feet landed on his head, we could hear his bones cracking. With every smash, huge volumes of poison spewed out of his mouth. Very soon, Kaliya was rid of all the poison in his body. Now when Sri Krishna continued to dance, it was blood that spurt out.

Though it was a wonderful dance performance and a great show for everyone around the lake, it was the greatest misery and pain for our husband Kaliya. We could see that he was dying. There was literally no strength left in his body. That look of arrogance was long gone and replaced by a look of humility that only an experience like this can bring. Our husband was no longer the arrogant demon that he used to be. Reality seemed to have dawned on him. He had understood the supremacy of Sri Krishna and the gravity of his mistakes. He was now repentant.

We felt that it was time for us to step out and try to save our husband. With folded hands and tear-filled eyes, we swam towards Sri Krishna who was still in the process of smashing whatever little pride was left in Kaliya. With great love and affection in our hearts, we glorified the Supreme Lord with chosen prayers composed in his glorification. We whole-heartedly supported the punishment the Supreme

Lord chose to give our husband Kaliya for torturing and killing so many of the residents of Vrindavan who were so dear to Sri Krishna. But along with that, we submitted a plea that he be forgiven since his pride had been vanquished. Touched by our heartfelt prayers, Sri Krishna jumped off our husband's head.

Kaliya was so weak by then that he could barely manage to raise even a single hood. But with great humility in his voice, he offered prayers of surrender to Sri Krishna offering his life and soul in Sri Krishna's service. He begged forgiveness for the unpardonable mistakes he had committed while in the holy land of Vrindavan. With tears of repentance streaming down his eyes, he again and again offered his prostrated respects to the Supreme Lord. We were ecstatic to see our husband finally become a devotee of the Supreme Lord. Gone was his pride and arrogance. He was filled with great devotion and humility now. It was such a pleasure to see such a powerful transformation right in front of our eyes. We realised that the Lord's punishment is also his kindness in a different way.

Showing great compassion, Sri Krishna accepted our prayers and chose to forgive Kaliya. But he also warned him that he shouldn't ever be seen around Vrindavan. Kaliya then explained the reason for his entering Vrindavan in the first place. Fear of Garuda, the carrier of Lord Vishnu, had led him to take shelter in this lake. This lake was the only place in the universe that Garuda could not enter. Shaubari *muni* had cursed the bird and banned him from entering the premises of this lake. Respecting the curse of the sage, Garuda never entered the vicinity of that lake from that moment. Knowing that lake to be the haven where he would be safe from the harassment of Garuda, Kaliya moved in with his family creating his own private world there.

Sensing Kaliya's fear of moving out of the safety of that lake once again, Sri Krishna reassured him of his safety. He told him that his footprints were on every head of Kaliya, doubling as a decorative tilak adorning his forehead. Garuda would not dare to touch him when he saw the marks of his master's lotus feet on them. Kaliya gratefully agreed to move out and as per Sri Krishna's instructions, we moved out of that lake via the Yamuna river and entered the great ocean, shifting to an island known as the Ramanaka island.

Even now we reside in a cave on that island constantly singing the glories of Sri Krishna along with the whole family. Kaliya has become a saint now, though he does look scary when he raises his thousand hoods. But no one is scared of him as he is a gentle soul who always speaks about the glories of Sri Krishna and Vrindavan *dham*. We worship our husband because he is so fortunate to have had the opportunity to experience the Supreme Lord's feet dancing on his head. Whenever we see the lotus feet marks on his head, we are reminded of his good fortune. Once in a while, Sri Krishna does remember Kaliya and calls him for a ride, especially when he wants to take the waterways instead of the airways of Garuda. We anticipate those special moments!

CHAPTER 16

WHEN MATHURA SIGHED WITH RELIEF

The journey from Mathura to Vrindavan was the greatest journey of my life. A multitude of emotions churned my heart. There was fear, there was concern, there was confusion, there was sorrow, there was hope, there was danger, and there was anger. But more than all of this, there was love. This was a journey I had taken millions of times in my heart during the last eleven-and-a-half years. From the moment I heard of Vasudeva Krishna's birth in Mathura jail and his eventual transference to Vrindavan, my heart had been yearning to go there. But my political duties and my loyalty to King Kamsa did not allow me to visit Vrindavan. Only my body was loyal to Kamsa; my heart was eternally loyal to Vasudeva Krishna.

Though I felt all those negative emotions in my heart, there was that one supreme positive emotion of love that simply escalated with the hooves of my sprinting horses moving closer to the holy land of Vrindavan. I immersed my mind totally in the divine stories of Vasudeva Krishna that I had heard for many years. The stories now seemed to be coming alive for me as I approached that holy land. Though I had a duty to perform there, I considered this trip nothing short of a pilgrimage.

I have seen many family feuds in my life, but none like this one. Vasudeva Krishna's maternal uncle, Kamsa, was desperate to kill him. And I was the one going to Vrindavan to fetch Vasudeva Krishna under the pretext of inviting him to Mathura so that Kamsa could finish him off. Although my name Akrura means one who is not cruel, this was the cruellest thing that I was doing in my life. Of course, I would do my best to save Vasudeva Krishna. I would tell him of Kamsa's evil plans. After that, Vasudeva Krishna would know how to best deal with his uncle. The moment my chariot entered the precincts of Vrindavan, I couldn't resist the desire to fling myself in the dust of Vrindavan. The very dust on which my Lord and Master Vasudeva Krishna walked every single day. In fact, as I rolled on the dust of that holy land, I could see the footprints of Vasudeva Krishna's lotus feet with sixteen divine markings.

Somehow composing myself, I steadied my mind and once again assumed the serious and sober look of the royalty of Mathura. My first vision of Vasudeva Krishna was mesmerising. For a few moments, I was speechless. Words failed me as his beauty captured my heart. Only when he shook me, was I able to come out of my reverie. I then conveyed the official and the unofficial message. The official message was that he, with his family and friends, was invited to Mathura by Kamsa for a grand *dhanusha yagya*, a ritualistic bow sacrifice. The unofficial message was that it was a ploy to kill him.

Vasudeva Krishna laughed heartily at this disclosure. I guessed the seriousness of the matter didn't register with him. Vasudeva Krishna informed mother Yashoda that he was leaving for Mathura the next day. The moment everyone heard the terrible news that he was leaving Vrindavan, there was a wail storm. The wail storm ravaged Vrindavan so badly that soon, from every direction in Vrindavan, all one could hear was the wailing and cries of agony. I had never realised that Vasudeva Krishna leaving Vrindavan would have such an impact on the Vrajvasis. It was heart-rending to see the cloud of gloom descending on them when they heard that the apple of their eye was leaving Vrindavan. Again,

I was the culprit in their eyes, taking their precious one away from them.

Gopis, gopas, uncles, aunts, cows, monkeys, and every possible living being from Vrindavan had gathered around Krishna, begging him not to leave. The one who was Vasudeva Krishna for me was Vrindavan Krishna for them. They had never ever imagined that he would also be known as Vasudeva Krishna one day. Seeing their state, Vrindavan Krishna consoled everyone individually and assured them that he would be back soon.

The next morning, we departed early. Nanda Maharaj along with an entourage from Vrindavan had departed long before us. Vasudeva Krishna and Balaram would be accompanying me because I felt I was responsible for their safety on the journey and this would be a great opportunity for me to be with Vasudeva Krishna. On the way, Krishna stopped the chariot so we could bathe in the crystal-clear waters of the Yamuna river in the outskirts of Vrindavan. While I waited in the chariot, the brothers proceeded to have their bath. When they returned to the chariot, I too requested permission to bathe in the holy waters of the Yamuna river to purify not just my body but my entire existence. With a smile, Vasudeva Krishna approved.

I was so absorbed in my thoughts of Vasudeva Krishna that I actually thought I saw him and Balaram in the water. Immediately I emerged out of the waters and checked the chariot. Lo and behold, there they were, sitting outside with a smile on their faces. I dipped my head in the water once again and this time I saw a fascinating scene. Not only were Vasudeva Krishna and Balaram there in the water, but they were also being elaborately worshipped by many celestial beings. Suddenly, with my own eyes, I saw Balaram turn himself into Seshanaag, the celestial serpent, and Vasudeva Krishna turn into Lord Maha Vishnu. I came out of the water in a daze. Had I really seen what I saw? It was fantastic. My hair was standing on end and I had goosebumps all over. When I returned to the chariot, I saw a mystical all-knowing smile on the faces of both the brothers. They were not looking at me but gazing towards the land of Mathura.

We soon reached our destination. When the citizens of Mathura heard of Vasudeva Krishna's arrival, they lined up in the streets for a glimpse.

The women, being shy, did not come out on the streets but went up to terraces to admire the handsome Vasudeva Krishna from afar. They were so eager that they abandoned what they were doing midway and ran recklessly to get a glimpse of him. Some of them rushed over with their makeup half done, with kajal in one eye and an earring in only one ear. Some were there wearing anklets on only one ankle. It was an amusing sight. Some brides had left their wedding rituals halfway just for the pleasure of feasting their eyes on Vasudeva Krishna. His arrival had turned Mathura into a mega festival.

I invited Vasudeva Krishna and Balaram to come home and rest for a bit, but they were more interested in seeing the city. They seemed to be intrigued by its tall gates and crystal arches. They smiled at the sound of peacocks and pet turtledoves. They whispered to each other pointing at the balconies and courtyards studded with diamonds, sapphires, pearls, and emeralds. They were fascinated by the city. This was their first visit to any city and for that matter, any place outside the simple village of Vrindavan.

Disappointed to part ways with them, I left to inform King Kamsa about their arrival. However, I was well-prepared with my own network of spies who would be keeping an eye on Vasudeva Krishna and Balaram and would keep me informed about their activities. So I was not really anxious about leaving them. Disappointed, yes. But they were safe for now. Not that I had any doubts. Who could harm the Supreme Lord? And who was I to save him?

After I was done with my duties, I awaited news from my spies. They soon arrived and updated me on the activities of Vasudeva Krishna and Balaram. From their flushed faces and wide eyes, I could make out they were in awe of the brothers.

"Honourable Sir," they addressed me, "Krishna and Balaram were strolling on the streets of Mathura when they bumped into a washerman carrying a basket full of colourfully dyed clothes. Krishna asked him to hand over the clothes to him in return for a handsome reward. But the washerman refused. He said the clothes were for royalty, not fit for commoners. The washerman's impudence really angered Krishna. He simply touched the washerman's neck with his finger and his head rolled off! Then Balaram and he calmly picked up some clothes from the basket and wore them and distributed the rest to the other boys."

Continuing the astonishing saga from there, another said, "Soon they bumped into a weaver. Unlike the washerman, this man offered them all that he had. He had woven wonderful ornaments which he gifted with total surrender. Krishna was mighty pleased and blessed him with material opulence, physical strength, and even liberation after death."

I was amazed at all the stories that I was hearing. Everything I had heard about Krishna was true. He lavished extravagant gifts and blessings to all who were devoted to him. Better to have a master like Krishna than Kamsa, I reflected. In serving Kamsa, I had wasted my life.

My thoughts jerked back to the present.

"They went to visit Sudama, the garland maker," whispered another of my men, "Sudama was ecstatic to see them. He prostrated on the floor immediately and worshipped them by offering garlands, sandalwood paste, and other exotic things. Pleased, Krishna granted him any benediction he desired but Sudama only had unflinching love and devotion for Krishna. This pleased Krishna even more and he gave him fame, strength, and prosperity as well."

We were all sharing our amazement at Vasudeva Krishna's lilas. The next encounter was even more baffling. "He then met a hunchbacked woman called Kubja. She offered all her beautifying ointments to Krishna so that he would appear the most beautiful. She said Krishna alone deserved the superlative ointments she had made. This gladdened Krishna's heart so much that he gave her an unforgettable gift. Kubja, who is called Trivakra because she was bent in three places, was in for a surprise. Krishna placed his foot on her toes and with his hands on her chin, he straightened her so that her hunchback disappeared and she transformed into a beautiful young damsel, quite like a caterpillar turning into a butterfly."

Every act of Krishna's was so enlightening. From the washerman and weaver incident, I realised that I should not be serving Kamsa but Krishna. From the Sudama episode, I learnt what boons to ask from Krishna—constant devotion for him and compassion for all living beings. From the Kubja episode it was clear that when Krishna enters your life, magic begins to happen.

The story continued, "Kubja invited Krishna home; Krishna agreed to visit her later. Saying goodbye to her with sweet words, the brothers walked to the dhanusha yagya arena. And they are there right now."

Just then we heard an ear-shattering sound. Something dramatic was going on. The sound was so terrorising that we trembled in fear. We rushed to the arena. We saw the massive bow neatly broken into two. Everyone was in shock, especially the guards. With the bow broken, the guards feared King Kamsa's anger and how he would punish them for negligence. Later, we came to know how Kamsa himself was filled with panic and alarm hearing the tumultuous sound as the vibrations filled the earth and sky.

As soon as the guards came to their senses, they pounced on Vasudeva Krishna and Balaram. The duo picked up the broken bow and wielded it like swords and killed all the guards. And then they coolly walked out of that arena, whistling in glee, without a care in the world.

It was evening now. The brothers walked out of the city gates and spent the night with their cowherd friends who had tents outside the city precincts. This was technically the last night that Vasudeva Krishna would spend with the Vrajvasis. No one at that time realised it but history has recorded it carefully.

While the brothers slept peacefully, Kamsa spent a sleepless night. He saw many omens that signalled his imminent death. He saw his reflection in his mirror but his head was missing. His shadow on the wall had a hole. The moon appeared double. Ghosts were embracing him. He dreamt that he was riding a donkey and drinking poison. With such graphic and ghastly dreams and omens, he spent the worst night of his life. Morning came and he sprang out of bed, determined to face Krishna and Balaram, and hopefully put an end to the saga that had been going on since the day Devaki got married and his death had been forecast. Not a single night had he slept in peace. Not a single day had he spent without anxiety. It was now or never. Krishna had to die today, he concluded.

I was getting news of Vasudeva Krishna as well as Kamsa from my sources. So far so good. I had warned Vasudeva Krishna and after my underwater vision on the outskirts of Vrindavan, I had no doubts whatsoever as to the outcome. Kamsa's days were numbered and Mathura would soon be free of his atrocities. I felt like a small boy wanting to clap my hands in sheer glee.

King Kamsa had announced a wrestling match to be held at the arena. His plan was to get Vasudeva Krishna to face his gigantic wrestlers. If necessary, he would let loose a mad elephant too to trample his enemy. Once Vasudeva Krishna entered the ring, he would not be allowed to leave alive. But little did he know that man proposes and God disposes.

The open amphitheatre was packed to capacity. Nanda Maharaj and his entourage were seated in the galleries in front. King Kamsa sat royally on his throne. The wrestlers, Chanura, Mushtika, and others sat, dressed ostentatiously, on a mat inside the ring. Everyone swayed to the beats of the loud music. Vasudeva Krishna and Balaram were conspicuous by their absence. Kamsa sent his guards to find them and bring them. He had strategically placed the mad elephant at the entrance so that he could trample Vasudeva Krishna even as he entered.

Vasudeva Krishna purposely arrived late to emphasise his total disobedience and uncaring attitude towards Kamsa's rule. But when he did, he found himself facing the wild beast. The elephant named Kuvalayapida wasn't an ordinary beast. It had the combined strength of hundreds of elephants. Vasudeva Krishna readied himself for a fight by taking off his jacket and tying it around his waist. He gathered his curly hair and tied it up neatly. He instructed the mahout to let them pass or be prepared to face Yamaraj, the god of death. However, the mahout, equally mad, urged his elephant to attack him. The elephant charged at him, wanting to crush the puny child under all of his ten thousand kilograms of weight. Vasudeva Krishna slipped under his trunk and hid behind his leg. The elephant could not see him.

I was at the entrance awaiting Vasudeva Krishna's arrival when this happened. I almost forgot to breathe but I immediately relaxed knowing Krishna's divine powers. The elephant, to me, represented the huge mass of ignorance that had to be destroyed to keep faith in Krishna alive within us.

However, this elephant was very much real and

trying to locate Krishna. Vasudeva Krishna caught hold of his tail and dragged him along as if he was dragging a small toy tied to a rope. In fact, the dexterity he showed in handling the elephant was a reflection of his expertise in herding cows. Vasudeva Krishna continued to display playful acrobatic skills like falling down and getting up, sometimes slapping the elephant, sometimes dodging him. Finally, when he had had enough of play, he got serious. He pulled his trunk and threw him on the ground. Climbing over him, he extracted his tusk and killed him as well as his keeper.

Vasudeva Krishna then made a grand entry into the arena, carrying the broken tusk over his shoulder, sprinkled with blood and sweat, adding masculine charisma to his handsome face. The citizens of Mathura gawked at him and admired him shamelessly. The women threw all caution to the wind and stared at him openly. Everyone was deeply intoxicated with his beauty. They discussed his valour and the demon-killing deeds that they had heard of. The entire stadium was immersed in Krishna *katha*. I was happy to see everyone in Mathura discussing Krishna so openly without fearing Kamsa. Chanura and Mushtika, who had also gone into a trance, snapped out of it and challenged Vasudeva Krishna and Balaram. The duo dashed towards them. Vasudeva Krishna and Balaram appeared minuscule and puny in front of the humungous wrestlers. The women wondered at the logic behind this unfair wrestling. How could two small boys ever defeat these professional, muscled wrestlers? The entire audience sympathised with the two boys. The audience screamed, "Unfair! Unfair!" and "go fight someone your own size."

Unfazed and unperturbed, Vasudeva Krishna reached his opponents and started a fist fight, while Balaram engaged with his palm. Both toppled their opponents without much ado. Chanura and Mushtika fell on the ground and Vasudeva Krishna and Balaram hit them on their heads and sent them to Yamaraj. It was all over in two minutes. A herd of wrestlers rushed to attack them but within minutes, they were history too.

Kamsa trembled in anger. He stopped the victory music and ordered his yes-men to throw the brothers out of Mathura. In a masterful stroke, before Kamsa could react, Vasudeva Krishna had jumped from the ring onto Kamsa's throne. Grabbing his sword and shield, he threw him on the floor. Positioning himself on his chest, he hammered and punched him until Kamsa vomited blood and life drained away from him. He dragged the dead body of Kamsa around to show the citizens that Kamsa was finished. Kamsa was finally dead! We were free! Vasudeva Krishna had done it! There was a loud cheer as everyone scrambled towards their hero. Carrying him on their shoulders, they did a victory lap.

I, for one, felt a huge burden lifted off my back. My tense body relaxed. After many decades, I was at peace. Now peace would prevail everywhere. Mathura would finally have a ruler she deserved. After eleven-and-a-half years, Vasudeva and Devaki were reunited with their child. The years of sacrifice did not go in vain. The pain and the hurt that Vasudeva and Devaki had carried in their hearts for so many years melted in the heat of their tears as they embraced their loving son Krishna to their hearts' content.

CHAPTER 17

Dwarkavasi:

THE MAKING OF DWARKA, A MYSTICAL CITY

Although I live in Dwarka now, I identify more with Mathura. That's because I was born and brought up in Mathura. I would have died there too, but for Yadunandana Krishna. To save the people of Mathura from Jarasanda, Yadunandana established the city of Dwarka in the middle of an ocean. Overnight, we were relocated. And saved. All glory to Yadunandana, our saviour.

I was an ordinary citizen of Mathura at the time. I still am. Kamsa had been killed and King Ugrasena wore the crown. All the citizens of Mathura, including me, were happy about it. Yadunandana Krishna and Balaram lived in Mathura too. It could have been a perfect life, but alas, it was not. Kamsa's wives, now widows, had gone back to their father and their father was livid! I understand a father's pain at having to see his daughters as pitiful widows. Yet, we had no sympathy for them because the person in question was the evil and cruel Kamsa. There was only one emotion we felt intensely when he died. Joy! We didn't care if the mighty King Jarasanda's daughters had been widowed. But Jarasanda did.

After all, he was the king of Kashi or Magadh. And he decided to avenge the death of Kamsa. Since Yadunandana Krishna was responsible for Kamsa's death, Jarasanda vowed to destroy the entire Yadu dynasty. Leading a strong army, he attacked Mathura. His army had twenty-three phalanxes, all comprising of thousands and thousands of chariots, soldiers, elephants, and horses and he deployed all his forces in surrounding the city of Mathura. Of course, King Ugrasena, supported by Vasudeva and his chief military strategist Akroor, along with Yadunandana Krishna and Balaram were ready to face the challenge. In fact, they did not even need an army. Yadunandana Krishna and Balaram were sufficient to foil any attack. When Yadunandana Krishna got into action, he was unstoppable.

Soon heads were rolling with severed heads of elephants, horses, and others flowing in a river of blood. What a ghastly sight it was! Balaram, with his expertise in wielding the club, added to the destruction and Jarasanda had to retract like a coward. Balaram pounced on him, ready to bind Jarasanda with a rope and take him as a prisoner of war. However, Yadunandana Krishna, who always had futuristic thinking, stopped him and released Jarasanda.

Jarasanda, ashamed of the defeat and worse still, the insult heaped on him, decided not to return to his kingdom but retire from the throne. But his friends prevailed upon him and convinced him that his defeat was sheer bad luck. If he gathered his resources again, he could salvage his pride and be victorious. Jarasanda agreed to forget this humiliation and returned to his kingdom.

Mathura was already celebrating the death of Kamsa and this victory over Jarasanda gave us more reasons to rejoice. But we did not expect this non-stop series of celebrations to continue. Because Jarasanda, inspired by his friends, did not stop after his first defeat. He put together another army of demons and came back. He kept attacking and Yadunandana Krishna kept packing them off as many as seventeen times. Yes, seventeen times. Boy, was Jarasanda dull! Some people never learn. He just wouldn't get the message. We didn't mind as every defeat meant more celebrations and Mathura was perpetually in festive mode thanks to Jarasanda, who returned home disappointed every time.

But what happened next was totally unexpected. Mathura was attacked not by one but by two kings simultaneously: Jarasanda (as usual) and Kalyavan, the king of Yavanas (a demonic tribe). Kalyavan attacked us at the same time Jarasanda made his eighteenth attempt. Kalyavan had a boon from Lord Shiva that he would never have to fear any of the Yadavas except for Yadunandana Krishna.

The double attack was worrisome. If we focused our forces on Kalyavan, Jarasanda would get the opportunity he was looking for to capture Mathura. If he managed to do that, he would vent his anger in the most gruesome way, killing all the Yadavas indiscriminately. Imagine the frustration level of a king defeated seventeen times and his joy in tasting victory the eighteenth time!

Yadunandana Krishna came up with a unique plan. He decided to build a fort, so protected that there was no way of entering it. It was to be situated in the middle of an ocean. That is how the city of Dwarka came into existence. Having done that and transported everyone to safety, he returned to Mathura. The plan was that he would take on Kalyavan and Balaram would engage with Jarasanda.

When Yadunandana Krishna came face to face with Kalyavan, instead of fighting the demon, Yadunandana Krishna left the battlefield and ran away from there. Kalyavan ran after him, determined to kill him. But who can catch the Lord of all living beings? Even though Yadunandana Krishna walked at a casual pace, Kalyavan could not catch up with him. He ran as fast as his demonic legs could carry him but no matter how fast he ran, no matter how much he huffed and he puffed, the elusive Yadunandana Krishna always remained out of reach.

If you think Yadunandana Krishna was running to save his life or because of his fear for Kalyavan, you're absolutely off the mark. He was a deep thinker with layers of strategies that no one else could think of. He headed straight to a cave in the nearby mountains. Now, why would he do that? That brings us to another tale. The tale of Muchukunda.

Muchukunda was a king from Treta *yuga*. Born in the Ikshvaku dynasty, he was an ancestor of Lord Rama. His name and fame as a valorous army commander had spread beyond earth and reached the heavenly planets. At that point, the gods were continuously locked in a battle with the demons, and without a commander to lead them, they were constantly at the losing end. To turn the situation around, Indra approached Muchukunda to lead them in their war against demons so that they could overpower their arch enemies.

Muchukunda agreed and reached the heavenly realms. There he led the gods in a fierce battle, which went on for many heavenly days. One heavenly day roughly equals to 365 earthly days. So, when the battle ended, lakhs of years had passed on earth and no one from Muchukunda's family survived. The gods, pleased with Muchukunda's selflessness in fighting the war for them, wanted to grant him any boon that he wanted. The war had taken a heavy toll on him and Muchukunda desired nothing but restful sleep. He felt he could sleep forever, if given an opportunity. Having no family left and nowhere to go, he asked for the boon of sleep. He wanted to sleep so badly that he added a condition to it that if anyone tried to wake him up against his wishes, he would turn them to ashes with a mere glance. The gods happily granted him the boon and Muchukunda finally retired to a cave for his much-needed rest.

If Kumbhakaran was known for his enormous

amount of sleep, Muchukunda was many notches higher than him. Not just years but yugas went by with him sleeping and refusing to wake up. Yadunandana Krishna thought it was time to wake Muchukunda up as he had slept enough. With this goal in mind, Yadunandana Krishna headed towards the cave where Muchukunda lay in deep slumber.

On reaching the inside of the cave, Yadunandana Krishna covered the sleeping Muchukunda with his own yellow garment and hid in a dark corner. Sure enough, Kalyavan entered the same cave, hot on the heels of Yadunandana Krishna. He saw Muchukunda covered in Krishna's yellow garment and mistakenly assumed him to be Yadunandana Krishna. Surprised that he had chosen to sleep instead of fight, he gave Muchukunda a hard kick. Startled and awakened before he desired, Muchukunda went wild. His angry red eyes looked at Kalyavan, emitting a flash of fire, and that was the instantaneous end of the demon. Kalyavan was now a heap of ashes on the floor. Yadunandana Krishna had killed two birds with one stone. Kalyavan had been effortlessly killed and Muchukunda had been awakened without any harm.

Yadunandana Krishna then appeared before him and blessed him with liberation. He also advised him to begin a life of austerities to wash off the sins accumulated from fighting the war. Muchukunda came out of the cave to realise that lakhs of years had passed and he was now in *Dwapar* yuga where the size of human beings had shrunk considerably. They appeared puny to him compared to his size. He proceeded to Badrika ashram to perform his meditation and attain liberation.

Next, Yadunandana Krishna and Balaram fled from the battle going on with Jarasanda. They escaped from the war zone by jumping off a mountain and reaching Dwarka fort. Overnight, he had already transported all the citizens of Mathura, including the birds and animals, to Dwarka. Dwarka was a safe haven. Surrounded by the ocean, no one would dare to attack them. A formidable army was constantly on guard to protect the city from any dangers lurking in the skies or waters. And thankfully, there were none.

Dwarka was like a dream city, designed and constructed by none other than the celestial architect Vishwakarma. Its area covered ninety-six square miles with its fortified walls having their base in the ocean. Everything about the city was picture-perfect—its symmetrical streets, dotted by Kalpavrikshas or desire-fulfilling trees imported from the spiritual world, its beautiful picturesque gardens and landscapes, its palaces and huge gates, its skyscrapers, the rooms inside every house with jewelled flooring and big golden pots—everything about Dwarka was nothing short of amazing. In the centre of the city stood the house of King Ugrasena, truly a joyous piece of architecture we all admired.

There was no longer any threat of attack from any direction. We were in the safe hands of Yadunandana Krishna and Balaram. When God wants to save you, no one has the power to harm you. And if God decides to kill you, no one has the power to save you. I have experienced this first-hand.

CHAPTER 18

Revati:

HOW KRISHNA HELPED ME TO MARRY LORD BALARAM

I am Revati. But in my last life, I was Jyotishmati, born out of a yagya *kunda* and then adopted by Manu. As Jyotishmati, there was no shortage of love and affection in my life. But alas, I reached the age when my father Manu thought I should get married. The question was, to whom? I was very clear about that. I could never marry an ordinary man. I would only marry someone who was strong and all-powerful. Nothing less than that!

Now the search began for the one who was capable enough to attract my heart. On earth, there are strong men but no one could claim to be the strongest. Neither could Indra, Vayu, or the other *devatas* in heaven stake a claim to that title. Who then was that one personality who possessed all the strength?

We finally concluded that it was none other than Lord Ananta who could hold the entire universe on just one of his hoods. Identifying the personality did not solve our problem. How does one approach Lord Ananta with a marriage proposal? My father had no clue. Neither did anyone else. He was out of reach even for devatas. He could be seen only when he wished to be. I was in a fix. I knew I wanted him as my life partner. I knew he was my dream partner. But I had no way of sending my message of love to him. Marrying him was like a distant dream.

The days were filled with turmoil. It is very difficult to nurture a broken heart. I was drifting into a world of loneliness, cutting off all contact with my near and dear ones, preferring to simply be alone with the pain of separation from my venerable Lord. Thankfully, those dreadful days did not last long and my father Manu, unable to see my grief, came up with a suggestion.

"Daughter, there is only one way to attract the mercy of Lord Ananta. And that is by means of austerities. If you are up to it, I recommend you take a vow of austerities following which you will surely attain your goal."

My eyes lit up. There was indeed a way out. However difficult it seemed, it was worth a try. I was determined to make it work somehow. I took my father's blessings and set out on the arduous road. I was rather excited. Something told me I was a step closer to my goal. It would take time, no doubt, but

I was on the right path. With hope in my heart and a prayer on my lips, my new life began.

However, I was not quite prepared for what followed. My sincere absorption in meditation attracted the devatas. Indra, Yama, Kubera, Agni, Varuna, Surya, Shukra, Shani, and a host of others queued up wanting my hand in marriage. It was a distraction that really got on my nerves. One by one, they would come and put forth their request. In spite of refusing their proposals and making it clear that I wanted only Lord Ananta, the message was not getting through to them. Here I was, trying to focus on my Lord but these devatas had an agenda of their own, hampering my penance. I could not control my wrath any further, and much to their shock, I heaped curses on all of them for interrupting my *sadhana*.

This did not go down well with the king of heavens, Lord Indra. He was livid that I had cursed them for no fault of theirs. They had not harmed me or cheated me in any way. Then why the curse?

"You could have simply refused our proposals," he argued, "instead of cursing innocent beings. I curse you that even after attaining Lord Ananta, you will not have the bliss of motherhood. Only when

Lord Ananta undoes the curses you heaped on us will your curse be reversed."

Although I was shaken by what he said, everyone knew that eventually, I did mother two handsome boys.

I continued my days with severe austerities and the glow of my body increased day by day. A time came when I was a ball of fire and Lord Brahma was in panic mode because the heat from my fire would destroy his creation. Seated on his swan, he immediately appeared before me and requested me to halt my austerities lest I turn everything into ashes.

"Your wish to attain Lord Ananta will not be fulfilled as of now. You will have to wait for the Vaivasvat Manvantara for Lord Ananta to appear in Dwapar yuga. I promise you that then, he will accept you as his partner. Till then, you can come and stay in my Brahmaloka."

I was ready to take birth again and again to attain my Lord. I was willing to burn in the fire of even more severe austerities. I was willing to wait till the end of time. As long as it pleased my Lord and he accepted me. I left with Lord Brahma.

The wheel of time turned and I was reborn as Revati in the dynasty of Vaivasvat Manu. King Kakudmin was my illustrious father, eldest son of King Revata in the line of King Anarta and King Sharyati. My father had performed a yagya because he had no child. And I was born as Revati. And once again, my father wondered who would be a suitable match for me, his exquisite daughter. Compelled by an inner voice, I suggested he visit Lord Brahma for advice. Lord Brahma would surely know who he had created for me. Seeing merit in the suggestion, he took me along and we went to Brahmaloka.

Inside the court, we found Lord Brahma immersed in the divine music of the gandharvas. When the music ended, he turned his attention towards us and my father put forth his request. Hearing that, Lord Brahma burst into laughter. He said, "Noble king, the few minutes passed in Brahmaloka have been equal to many yugas on earth. By the time you return, all the eligible men you know will have been wiped out by time."

My father went numb hearing that. But Lord Brahma had not forgotten his promise. He said, "O' King, please return to earth and go to Madhupuri.

There you will find an earring-clad, plough-carrying, mace-wielding, golden-hued boy dressed in blue. He is the personification of Lord Ananta. He is the groom you are looking for." We wasted no time in leaving Brahmaloka.

Lord Ananta was at the banks of River Yamuna with his brother. They were surprised to see two huge figures descending from the sky. Compared to their size, we were gigantic. Both of us stood facing them. Far from being startled, Lord Sankarshan asked for our introduction. Nothing ever surprised the two brothers.

"I am King Kakudmin, son of King Revata from the first Satya yuga of this Manvantar," said my dignified father, "and this is my daughter Revati born from a yagya kunda. Lord Brahmaji has ordered me to give my daughter's hand to you in marriage. Please accept this proposal."

Before anyone could say anything, Lord Krishna spoke. "O' illustrious king, we are fortunate to accept your daughter's hand in marriage for my brother. I accept the proposal on his behalf."

What? Was I really hearing those words of acceptance? This was too good to be true. Lord

Krishna did not give his brother a chance to speak. He had immediately accepted the proposal as if he had been waiting for us to come. Lord Balaram raised no objections. Such was their bonding.

Happily, my father gave my hand to Lord Balaram and announced that he would now spend his days in the Himalayas doing penance. "My presence in the wedding will create inconvenience and I would not want that."

He was right. Even the tallest of the trees of Dwapar yuga only reached his knees. How would they accommodate him during the wedding? How would they serve him? Not that he would even accept a drop of water here. He departed immediately.

After he left, Lord Krishna said, "Brother, just look at sister-in-law's huge size." And he laughed rather hysterically.

"Wait a minute," responded Lord Balaram. He picked up his divine plough and placed it on my shoulder. What was on his mind? Applying pressure, he pushed the plough down. As the plough went down, so did I. Suddenly I was no longer looking down at them. I was, in fact, looking up at them. He had re-sized me! I now reached his ears. My jewellery, clothes, and everything had re-sized to fit my body. I turned red with embarrassment.

Lord Krishna was now running off to spread the news of this alliance. I felt a wave of gratitude for Lord Krishna. It was he who had readily accepted me. And Lord Balaram had mutely accepted Lord Krishna's acceptance. I was overwhelmed by the sudden turn of events. I had reached my destination. Gargacharya fixed the wedding date. There was exhilaration in the air. I heard that for the first time, Lord Krishna was excited about something. He personally supervised all the arrangements. I will always be thankful to him for the kindness he bestowed on me. I was finally a part of this divine family.

CHAPTER 19

Draupadi:
Saved in the Nick of Time

*S*ome people feel happy when they have more than others. Then there are those who are not content with having more, but enjoy seeing others miserable and envious of their wealth. One such person was Duryodhan. He was restless and perturbed that we were in good spirits and as happy as city dwellers, despite living in the jungle. He could not bear that in the forest too, Yudhishthir Maharaj fed many brahmans before he ate. After having usurped our kingdom, he desired to further see us living in misery. Our happiness in the forest was making him miserable!

Duryodhan was my brother-in-law, the brother of the Pandavas, my husbands. But in reality, he was our sworn enemy. His only purpose in life was to see us traumatised and he tried every trick in the book to accomplish that. It is only by the mercy of Achyuta that I am alive to tell you this story. Duryodhan snatched our kingdom from us, cheated in gambling, stooped low enough to disrobe me in public, tried to kill my husbands and my mother-in-law Kunti by burning all of them in a house of lac, tried to poison the mighty Bhima . . . the list is endless. My blood boils when I think of the series of sufferings in our lives because of one man's ego and atrocities. At the same time, I'm grateful that we always survived the ordeals somehow. By divine will. Achyuta has always been our saviour. He is the infallible one. My saviour.

At the time of this story, we were in the twelfth year of exile. Duryodhan, being Duryodhan, decided to rejoice in our austere lifestyle by having an opulent picnic just opposite our humble abode in the jungle. However, his plan for enjoyment backfired when he got into a tussle with Arjuna's friend, a gandharva called Chitraratha. Chitraratha would have finished him off then and there, had Arjuna not intervened and begged Chitraratha to forgive his brother Duryodhan. Karna had already made a hasty escape and left Duryodhan to fend for himself, knowing that he was no match for Chitraratha. I wonder why he was compared to Arjuna. He lacked both the courage and character. Anyway, although Duryodhan's friend Karna had disappeared from the scene, Arjuna appeared to save his unworthy brother.

Duryodhan shamelessly returned to Hastinapur, only to continue planning the downfall of the Pandavas in consultation with his like-minded Shakuni uncle, Karna, and other cronies. Since we were almost at the end of our exile, his insecurities were escalating. What if the kingdom slipped out of his hands? What if Yudhishthir became king?

In the middle of all this, a surprise visitor entered Hastinapur. Maharshi Durvas. And he was not alone. Ten thousand disciples accompanied him. Duryodhan's crooked mind saw an opportunity in this. If he could please the exalted muni with his servile attitude, his job would be done. On the other hand, if he did not serve him well, then he would have to bear the brunt of his curse. His sinister mind jumped into action and day and night, he served Durvas muni endlessly to please him.

Now let me tell you that Durvas muni was not an easy sage to please. He was pretty much unpredictable. He arrived at any time for meals and could not tolerate even a moment's delay. Sometimes, as soon as the food was served, he would walk out saying he was not hungry. Further, he made impossible demands at the spur of the moment. Be it noon or midnight. He didn't care. But Duryodhan was on high alert, always ready at his service.

Meanwhile, he was constantly in discussion with his uncle regarding what benediction he should ask for in case Durvas muni offered one at the end of his stay. If he was pleased, all his anxieties could be taken care of. If not, he was in for some curses.

Finally, the much-awaited day arrived. Durvas muni prepared to depart and being highly pleased, he instructed Duryodhan to ask him for any boon. "I am very happy with your intense desire to serve me. Ask me for anything."

Duryodhan, with folded hands, bending low, very humbly said, "I am grateful for the opportunity to serve you. I would like my eldest brother Yudhishthir to have this same opportunity as me. I would like you and your disciples to visit him as well. But pray, I have only one request. Please go there only when they have finished their meal and Draupadi has cleaned the vessels."

"I will do as you wish," assured the muni.

As soon as he departed, Karna shook hands with Duryodhan, gleeful at the successful execution of their plan. They all knew why Duryodhan had made that condition of going when I was resting after my meal. It was because of the inexhaustible vessel we had, the *Akshaya patra*, given to us by Lord Surya. It so happened that when we started for the forest, thousands of brahmans moved with us, unable to bear the separation from Yudhishthir Maharaj. Yudhishthir Maharaj pleaded with them to return citing numerous reasons, including the fact that he would be unable to feed so many of them. He did not want to burden his brothers and me by expecting us to procure food and cook for tens of thousands of people. But the brahmans were adamant about staying.

Disheartened, Yudhishthir Maharaj asked his guru Dhaumya to show him a way out. Guru Dhaumya suggested that Surya being the source of all food in the material world, would be the best person to help him. "Meditate on Lord Surya and ask him to rescue you."

Yudhishthir Maharaj did exactly as he was told. Gladdened by his focused sadhana, Surya appeared to grant his wish and bestowed upon him a mystical vessel—the Akshaya patra—that would provide us with a constant supply of food until I finished eating for the day and washed the vessel. Yudhishthir Maharaj put this Akshaya patra under my care so that I could do the needful. The catch was that once I had eaten and washed the vessel, the vessel would not supply any more food until the next day. Taking advantage of this fact, Duryodhan had attached that condition and Durvas muni, unknowingly, had fallen for it.

While celebrating their success in conniving against us and cheating us, they forgot the obvious. That the Pandavas have the shelter of the God of all gods. No one has the audacity or the capacity to harm those he shelters. Achyuta never lets down those under his shelter. It has never happened in the past and will never happen in the future. Thus, their joy was only short-lived.

The day Durvas muni arrived, the Pandavas had already fed all the brahmans. They had also eaten and soon after, I also ate. The Akshaya patra's job was done for the day. I had washed the vessel as part of my routine. I was resting when I heard the arrival of Durvas muni with his ten thousand disciples. Yudhishthir Maharaj hurried to welcome him. He washed his feet and offered him the highest seat.

The sage said, "O' king, we are hungry. We are going to the lake for a bath and after that please arrange for our meals."

Yudhishthir accepted his request and informed me. I now had to prepare to feed ten thousand and one hungry mouths. I nearly fainted. It was an impossible task. The gifted vessel could only be used once in a day and I had already used it. There was no way I could provide for even one more person, leave alone ten thousand and one. I also knew about Durvas muni's anger. He would waste no time in cursing us if we did not accede to his desires. This was a sure shot disaster for us. I braced myself for the worst calamity of my life.

Frankly, it's difficult to pick just one as the worst calamity of my life. Dushasan trying to rob my dignity in public would easily top the list. If I survived that, I could survive anything. So, collecting my nerves, I began to do what I always do in my most trying moments. Pray to my friend and well-wisher Achyuta.

I raised my hands up in the air and closed my eyes thinking of Achyuta. His handsome face danced in front of my mind's eye. For a moment I forgot all my problems and swam in the bliss of this vision. His eyes twinkled and his mouth crinkled into a smile. I forced myself out of the trance and called out loud, "O' Achyuta, you are the shelter of every devotee and destroyer of every evil. Please come and protect me. I have no one but you to ask for help. Please come and rescue me from the unprecedented anger of the great sage. Please save me from this extraordinary situation."

I said this again and again till my lips dried, my voice faltered, and my knees gave way. I fell on the floor in agony. I opened my eyes to the vision of a chariot driven by Daruka carrying my Achyuta. The king of Dwarka was in a hurry. He rushed out of the chariot and headed straight to me.

"Krishne, where are you?" he called out to me. He always addressed me as Krishne, because I too was dark like him. By then I was on my feet, ready to tell him my problem. But before I could utter a word, he told me his problem.

"Krishne, I'm very hungry. Please give me something to eat quickly! As quickly as you can!"

My jaw fell. Had he come to compound my problem?

"Achyuta, I have to feed ten thousand people with my empty Akshaya patra. And now you are hungry too? How can I feed you?" I cried helplessly. Achyuta was hungry and I was so unfortunate I had nothing to give him. Tears ran down my cheeks.

"Krishne, here I am dying of hunger and you cry? How mean is that? Feed me first and then feed your other thousands of guests."

I tried to explain, "Achyuta, the Akshaya patra has been washed and kept away. There is no food for anyone."

I went into the cooking area and got it out to show him the proof. "See, it's empty." I sobbed as I said.

This was worse than Durvas muni's curse. I felt so wretched and useless. For the first time, Achyuta had actually asked me for something and I wasn't able to help him.

Achyuta searched the vessel and suddenly his eyes lit up. He lifted a green leafy leftover of a vegetable hidden inside the vessel.

"Look what I found," he exclaimed, excited, holding the leaf up for me to see. I was wondering what lila he was going to perform now. He was in the mood for drama.

Once I saw the leaf, he promptly put it in his mouth dramatically, as if it was equivalent to the fifty-six opulent offerings he was used to daily. Not only that, he burped in contentment soon after and rubbed his stomach. I stared at him without blinking my eyes, lest I miss the climax. He went to the Pandavas and told Bhima, "Please call Durvas muni now for lunch. Tell him we are waiting."

What was he doing? I had no idea what he was up to. But knowing him to be Achyuta, the infallible one, I knew there was some reliable plan in his mind.

Meanwhile, at the lakeside, Durvas muni and his disciples were offering their prayers and chanting, standing in water. Suddenly, all of them felt bloated. They belched loudly, as if they had overeaten. How would they put another morsel of food down their throats? Just then Bhima appeared, to invite them. As soon as Durvas muni saw him, he panicked. It would be impossible to eat a single bite. But how could he refuse to eat after he himself had instructed Yudhishthir to prepare a meal for ten thousand disciples?

He told his principal disciples to start running away from Bhima. "If we go with him and don't eat, we will incur the wrath of the Lord. The incident of King Ambarish is fresh in my mind. I had angered him, which in turn angered the Lord, and I had to somehow save myself from death. Knowing that the Pandavas are devotees of Lord Hari, I don't want to be in a similar situation once again. The Sudarshan Chakra will surely find me if we are found guilty of wasting food for ten thousand people. Hurry. Let's hide from the ever-angry Bhima."

And the entire entourage hurried in the direction opposite to our camp. Bhima found the lake empty and no trace of any sage or his disciples. He heard from some observers that the entire group left fearfully in a hurry.

Bhima returned. Yudhishthir Maharaj was not convinced that the muni would not return. "He is unpredictable. He can even come at midnight and ask for the meal."

"No, he will not come back," Achyuta spoke with confidence, "Draupadi called me for help and I always come when someone is in need. Durvas muni will not feel any hunger now."

When the Supreme Lord is full, then how can any other creature in the universe feel hungry? When

Achyuta ate a little leaf, every living being's hunger was simultaneously satiated. My hero had rescued me once again. I watched him depart on his chariot and continued to gaze long after he had disappeared from sight. He still lingered on my mind.

CHAPTER 20

Satyabhama:

HOW I NEARLY LOST MY HUSBAND

Devrishi Narada's question was firmly stuck in my mind, refusing to let go. Did he not know that I, Satyabhama, was unlike other women? I was strong, with a mind of my own. I knew what I wanted in life and Dwarkadhish Krishna never undermined my desires. He was always ready to do anything for my happiness. Yet, Narada muni had doubted me. Nay, he had challenged me. His exact words still resounded in every fibre of my being, "Devi, do you have enough rights over Dwarkadhish to give him away in charity?"

I had given him a fitting reply. I would settle this once and for all. Today itself. Today I would confirm whether Dwarkadhish really meant what he said to me. If he was really mine. Not that I doubted it. But others did. That was equally insulting. I would set the record straight.

Night came and I accosted Dwarkadhish as soon as he entered our private chamber, "You always say that you are mine, but—"

"But what?" Dwarkadhish laughed at my query. His curly hair was blowing gently in the breeze giving him a boyish charm that made my heart flutter. His eyes danced merrily as he looked into my eyes, curious to know my innermost thoughts.

"If I donate you in charity, would that be acceptable to you?" I said with a straight face. I knew it sounded quite insane. Which wife would give away her husband in charity? But it was only a formality. Narada muni had explained to me that it would be extremely auspicious for me if I could pull this off. And it was only symbolic because he would not accept my charity and return Dwarkadhish back to me. So, I had nothing to lose and everything to gain. That is, if Dwarkadhish cooperated. And that was where Narada muni doubted my capabilities.

"Why don't you try me?" Dwarkadhish replied, sending me to blissful heights of ecstasy. There! Dwarkadhish would do anything for me. He said further, "Did you not get the Kalpataru in the same way?"

I proceeded to tell him my plans. I would invite Narada muni tomorrow and also invite several other family members to witness this event. I would need the Kalpataru too. I would organise a big festival and I would give away Dwarkadhish in charity. I would personally go to all my sisters who were Dwarkadhish's wives and take their permission for the donation. It would be a grand event. Dwarkadhish listened to me with his full attention and agreed to everything. I was in seventh heaven.

The next day, everything went well as per my plan. I had the permission of all my sisters to go ahead. I knew they would not object. I myself sent a personal invitation to Kunti Devi, Subhadra, Draupadi, and Gandhari. Also, on my list were Dhritarashtra, the Pandavas, Vidura, Bhishma, Duryodhan, Shishupal, and Rukmi. I could conveniently invite all of them because we were not in Dwarka but in Kurukshetra. Everyone was camped here. And Narada muni had already been sent a message.

I welcomed Narada muni as per protocol. I served him a sumptuous meal fit for the gods. As per etiquette, I took my sisters' permission in front of him. They gave their blessings profusely. I garlanded Dwarkadhish and tied him to the Kalpataru. But the Parijat tree shrank so much that it seemed as though I had tied the tree to Dwarkadhish's feet.

I chanted the mantras necessary to complete the donation. Then I sprinkled water over him to seal it. I also donated a thousand cows and innumerable gold coins to Narada muni. The gods showered flowers from above. Conches blew and the atmosphere was vibrant with music.

Narada muni stood up with his veena and addressed Dwarkadhish, "O' Keshav, Queen Satyabhama has given you away in charity to me. Now you belong to me. Please follow me and do as I say."

Dwarkadhish very humbly stood up and said, "Yes, I will."

I requested Narada muni to let me know how much I had to offer him to get Dwarkadhish back. Because that was the deal. That it would only be a symbolic donation. And once I offered him a suitable price, he would return my husband to me. But his answer gave me a heart attack. I could not believe his words.

"Devi, as you can see, I am detached to worldly riches. I have distributed the wealth of cows and gold coins that you gave me." He became very serious then and said, "You have given me the

Kalpataru, which has the power to give me whatever wealth or fame I need. And I give it all back to you. Please accept it as *prasad* from me. But how can I return the one who is not achievable by austerities and sadhana for many lifetimes? How can I possibly return him?"

Oh God! What was he saying? He was going back on his word. His words created panic in me and a sensation among the guests. Till now what had been simply a formality had taken on a strange twist. A very scary twist.

Again, I tried to clarify, "Did you not say that Uma had also given away her husband similarly in charity to you?"

"Yes, that's true, Queen Satyabhama," Narada replied gravely, "Mother Aditi had also donated Rishi Kashyap in the same way. I had returned them as per my word. And accepted a very insignificant number of cows, gold, and some sesame seeds."

My heart soared. I gushed, "Oh, I'll be more than happy to offer the same to you!"

But Narada muni was in no mood to listen to my pleas. In fact, he was upset. "You cannot force me to return what you have donated. It is now my right to do with it as I please. I am free to decide. When mother Aditi had tied Rishi Kashyap to Kalpataru, it did not shrink in size. Neither did it shrink when Parvati Devi tied her husband to it. And everyone saw what happened when Dwarkadhish was tied to it."

I was devastated. There was nothing left to say because technically, he was right. I could not possibly demand to take back what I had given in charity. I'm sure all my sisters were now regretting giving me permission to carry out this unusual act. I couldn't blame them. It had started out as a challenge for me to show that Dwarkadhish would never undermine my wishes but it was ending tragically with me losing everything. My very life, my Dwarkadhish. I was also bearing the brunt of all my sisters' anger on top of it all. How would I ever face them? I began to sob loudly.

Narada muni's next statement gave me some hope.

"I do not want to return Dwarkadhish at any cost, but your distress is unbearable. There is one way you can have him back. Please place him on a balance and give me anything worth his weight."

His words were like nectar, reviving me back into action. However, I saw Rukmini's reaction. She put her hands on her head and muttered something that sounded as though it was impossible to weigh Dwarkadhish's worth in jewels. I ignored her as I usually did. Narada muni had given me a ray of hope and I was going to grab it. I instantly ordered assistants to bring a weighing scale. I ordered my personal helpers to open my wardrobe and bring every jewel that I owned. Not only that, I asked for the royal treasury to deliver everything they had. We piled it all onto the scale. Even the Pandavas, Bhishma, and Rukmi emptied their treasures on the scale. Losing Dwarkadhish was not a calamity for me alone. Everyone was in a similar state at the thought of losing their very own Dwarkadhish. And I was like a daughter to all of them. They would do anything to allay my suffering.

But alas, even after everyone had contributed their wealth, the pan holding Dwarkadhish did not move even an inch above the ground. What should I do now? My mind was blank. I had tried every avenue. And failed miserably. My mind flashed back to Rukmini's reaction. She had known this would fail. Did she know something that I did not? Unlikely. She was not really the kind of person that one turned to in times of crisis. But clearly, she had known that weighing Dwarkadhish would not work. There was no harm in asking her. Drastic times called for drastic measures, I reasoned. Against my better judgement, and with no other option left, I fell at her feet.

"Sister, all the rishis glorify you. Please help me today to get our husband back." I pleaded with tears in my eyes.

She was crying too. As I had expected, she said, "I am a lowly servant of you and Dwarkadhish. Even if I sit myself, the scale will not move. But yes, there is something you can do. Call someone from the Vraj camp. Anyone from Vraj will know what to do."

Oh my God! I nearly fell unconscious. I had committed a gross error in not inviting anyone from the Vraj camp. Vrajvasis were here too, in Kurukshetra, in another camp. I myself ran on foot and fell at the feet of Radharani. It was totally my fault for not inviting her. Radha gently raised me up and hugged me tight. She heard my dilemma and with slow, firm steps she walked out. She reached our camp and ordered all the jewels to be cleared from there. Having done that, she plucked a Tulsi leaf from a garland around her neck and placed it on the scale.

To the astonishment of everyone present there, the pan carrying the Tulsi hit the ground and the pan carrying Dwarkadhish went up as if emptied out.

Narada muni instantly cried out, "Keshav, you are now free!"

He leapt to the weighing scale and grabbed the Tulsi leaf with great ferocity, as if afraid that he would lose it otherwise. He tucked it in his matted hair and danced ecstatically.

There was a wave of relief all around as the disaster was finally averted.

Many days later, I asked Narada muni the reason behind his ecstasy. He explained, "Tulsi represents Kirtikumari, Srimati Radharani herself. By offering Tulsi, Radha had offered herself. You had only given me Dwarkadhish but by Radha's mercy, I received both, Radha Krishna forever."

I learnt many valuable lessons. From Narada muni, from Radharani and from Rukmini. Never again would I underestimate the power of love and devotion. I had a long way to go to be anything like them.

CHAPTER 21

Vidura's
Wife Devika:

PEELS OF LOVE

adhav was expected to arrive in Hastinapur the next day. As soon as I heard this news, I got busy. Madhav in Hastinapur meant he would be coming to my house for sure. My husband Vidura was the only person he loved in Hastinapur. Of course, second only to the Pandavas. He would not accept hospitality anywhere else. He would surely come home for a meal if he had the time to eat.

I was right about that. I heard from our messengers that Madhav met Duryodhan at his palace and as expected, he had been extended an invitation to stay there for lunch. But Duryodhan had received an answer that he would never forget.

He said, "Suyodhan, there are only two reasons to accept food from others. One is out of love and the other is in case I am very hungry. Neither do I have any love for you, nor is there an emergency for me to eat."

And he did not stop at that. He was in the mood to speak out his heart. He said, "The Pandavas always adhere to religious principles. They have always wished for your well-being, unlike you who has always carried unnecessary hatred and envy in your heart for them. But remember this. If you hate them, you hate me as well. If you resent them, you resent me as well. Do not consider me separate from the righteous Pandavas."

And then, as a parting shot, he added, "Because you are always in wicked association, your food is unfit for consumption. At the moment, I will accept food only from Uncle Vidura in Hastinapur."

I was thrilled to hear his words. I basked in the warmth of his sentiments. I appreciated him all the more because he never hesitated to call a spade a spade. He chucked diplomacy and used plain cold words to get across his point. Fearless and precise. He never beat around the bush.

I can imagine how Duryodhan must have reacted to this but Madhav didn't care. In fact, I learnt that he did not even bother to escort Madhav to his chariot. Madhav mounted his chariot unescorted and left.

I had been busy all morning. Scrubbing the entire house till it sparkled. Decorating the house with flowers to create an ambience that Madhav would love. Cooking all kinds of delicious dishes for Madhav. I had to do everything myself because I did not trust my helpers to do it well enough. He would be arriving any minute now. I knew that the residents of Hastinapur must have lined up along the streets to catch a glimpse of him. But I was waiting for him at home where I could admire him to my heart's content.

He must have met Dhritarashtra now . . .

He must be paying obeisance to Grandfather Bhishma now . . .

He must be on the way home with my husband Vidura now . . .

I was counting every minute leading to his arrival.

"Aunt Devika, Aunt Devika!" I heard a voice call out. I did not have to guess who it was. I have known this voice from many births. Daruka's chariot had appeared at my door and Madhav got off.

His call . . . is heard through many, many lifetimes, at the most precious moments in life. Although he calls periodically, the material being is more attuned to the words of the world than his voice. His voice is heard only when the living being rises above his body, mind, and intelligence and is absorbed in the

Supreme Lord's lotus feet. As soon as I heard his voice, I ran towards the door. I forgot what I was doing. I had no consciousness of my physical body. All I knew was that Madhav had arrived. As soon as I opened the door, he removed his peacock feather crown and placed it on my head.

"Aunt Devika, I'm starving." He walked in and pulled a seat for himself. He was the same person who had lost his appetite on seeing the royal spread of food at Duryodhan's palace but was famished now after reaching the house of his devotee Vidura. But this ocean of love is never hungry for food; he is only hungry for love . . . only those who surrender at his lotus feet know this.

As soon as I saw him, I lost all my senses. I was neither conscious of myself nor was I aware of the world around me. In this condition, I had no recollection of what I had prepared for him. I saw a bunch of bananas and I sat down to feed him those. I was peeling the bananas lovingly and was so absorbed in my venerable Lord sitting in front of me that I was throwing the banana pulp away and feeding him the peels! Immersed in transcendental bliss, I was ignorant of my senseless actions. I could see Madhav relishing whatever I gave him and that was enough joy for me.

"How delicious!" He kept saying, every time I offered him the peels!

The topmost yogi also had no consciousness of what he was eating. He never needs to eat but when his devotee feeds him with so much love, he also loses his senses. He ate as if he was hungry since many lifetimes. Relishing every morsel of the banana peel.

I came out of my reverie suddenly with the arrival of my husband. He had learnt that Daruka's chariot had left the palace and was heading towards his home and had rushed home immediately. The door was open. As soon as he entered and saw me feeding banana peels to the Lord, he yelled at me in disgust, "What are you feeding to our Lordship?"

I was startled. He grabbed the bananas from my hands and said, "I will feed him now."

He sat down and offered the banana pulp to him. Madhav ate it, smiled cheekily and said, "It is not as tasty as the delicious peels."

Vidura was overwhelmed with emotion. In a choked voice he said, "I know what you like. The immense love you found in her is missing from my heart."

Vidura helped Madhav wash his hands and offered him a suitable place to sit. Then he worshipped him as per protocol. Touching his feet, he said, "By your presence, this house has become a holy place. My ancestors have been redeemed. By accepting my hospitality, you have blessed me."

As they were discussing the events that were leading to war, we had some visitors. Grandfather Bhishma, Dronacharya, Kripacharya, and some other kings from the neighbouring kingdoms arrived to meet Madhav. They all offered their opulent palaces for him to stay but Madhav refused them saying he was very comfortable here.

Once they had left, Vidura opened his innermost thoughts to Madhav. He said, "Madhav, it is better you go away without giving Duryodhan your peace proposal. He has no wisdom or a sense of discrimination of right from wrong. Even though you are thinking of his well-being, he will refuse your offer. He believes he can win the war if Karna supports him. Thus, he is not in a mood to compromise. He wants the entire kingdom for himself." Vidura was convinced that Duryodhan would reject his offer and he would stoop low enough to insult Madhav as well. He wanted Madhav to leave rather than face any of this.

"I know you are right," Madhav replied in agreement, "but I still have to make one attempt to get them on the right track. Even if Duryodhan refuses my offer, I will save myself from fools who will point fingers at me later saying that I could have avoided the war by compromising but I chose not to due to my antipathy for Duryodhan."

His reasoning made sense. Vidura remained silent as Madhav prepared to retire for the day. Tomorrow would be a new day. Whatever Madhav did, would be in the best interest of all. That much we were sure of.

CHAPTER 22

Ashwathama:

MY SHATTERED DREAM

While everyone in Hastinapur, including Duryodhan and his cronies, was thinking about who Madhusudan would stand with in the war, I had other pressing matters on my mind. In my opinion, Madhusudan's decision was a no-brainer. His love for the Pandavas was an open affair and I had no doubt that he would stand by them. He had always been there for them during the twelve years of exile and one year of obscurity. Duryodhan's adamance in not giving the kingdom to the Pandavas had already fuelled Madhusudan's anger. No, that was not my concern at all.

My bigger concern was what role I would play in the war. Being the son of Dronacharya, I naturally deserved to be at the forefront. Father would most likely be appointed commander-in-chief. There was no greater warrior than him. However, being old, he might not accept that position. Which meant I, Ashwathama, son of the great Dronacharya, would be the next automatic choice for commander-in-chief of the massive Kuru army. The very thought sent a shiver down my spine. I was excited and nervous at the same time. Bhishma was too old to be of any use. And Karna? He was a non-entity, a coward. All air and no substance. He only knew how to talk big and boast about himself. I had no competition, so to speak.

But there was another thought trying to make itself heard from somewhere deep within the recesses of my subconscious mind even as I was trying to bury it back. It was a disturbing thought and I really didn't want to face it. However hard I tried, it refused to be cowed down and soon it was the topmost thought nagging me. Again, it was about Madhusudan. I was confident of giving Arjuna a good fight, but was I good enough to defeat Madhusudan? His *Sudarshan Chakra* was unbeatable. No one had ever been able to overpower this unique weapon he possessed. I had even seen the speed with which it had severed the head of Shishupala in one swift movement during the Rajyasuya sacrifice of Yudhishthir. It was a scary thought. I, the future commander-in-chief of the Kuru army, was powerless against the mighty Sudarshan Chakra.

One thought led to another and soon I was wondering, *what if Madhusudan did not have the*

Sudarshan Chakra with him at time of war? What if the Chakra belonged to me instead? I was now excited about the possibility of the Chakra being in my possession and not his. What an awesome idea. I was floating in the dream of having the divine weapon at my disposal and conquering the world. I would have the Chakra in my hands and I would defeat Madhusudan! My fan-following grew larger by the minute. Who else but the son of Dronacharya deserved to have it? If I had the Chakra, Duryodhan would have no hesitation in appointing me the army commander. In fact, he would humbly grovel before me to cajole me to accept the post. My father, Bhishma, and Karna would be placed behind whereas I would lead from the front.

I was in a frenzy now. Overcome by a mad desire to somehow hold the Sudarshan Chakra in my hand and intoxicated by my surreal desires, I sat in my chariot and headed for Dwarka. I was a brahman. I would make use of that position. I had the perfect plan in my mind to usurp the Sudarshan Chakra and then kill Madhusudan himself with it in the war. I rubbed my hands in glee. This was fantastic.

I reached Dwarka. I was known there and

no one stopped me at any point. Even otherwise, Dwarka was well-known for welcoming all brahmans. The gatekeepers were more than happy to guide me to my destination.

I stayed for a few days in Dwarka waiting for an opportune moment with Madhusudan. I didn't have to wait too long as one day I was invited to the palace by Madhusudan. He went through the formalities of welcoming a brahman and offered me a sumptuous meal. Having done with all of that, he said, "I am most fortunate that you have sanctified my home with your presence. How can I serve you?"

I wasted no time. I said, "I have come with a request. You are a large-hearted king who gives away everything in charity to brahmans. Your fame as a well-wisher of brahmans has brought me to your doorstep." I hesitated to speak further.

"Please tell me what I can do for you," he encouraged me to open my heart.

I went in for the kill. "I want your divine Sudarshan Chakra. In return, you can take my Brahma *astra*." There! I had said it! Now what would he do? My heart was palpitating so fast I could feel it in my mouth. Would he accede to my wishes or would he throw me out of Dwarka? It was a moment of the greatest anxiety in my life. Moreover, if he agreed, I would lose my precious Brahma astra. I had got possession of it with great difficulty.

My own father who could have easily handed it over to me without a fuss chose not to. He gifted it to Arjuna, but not to me! How could he turn against his own son? I could never understand why he did what he did. But I was no less. I insisted that if he could give the Brahma astra to an outsider then why not to his own son? He gave me his usual sermon on being deserving first but I ignored all that. I deserved it simply because I was his son, didn't I? What other qualification was required beyond that? Eventually, he caved in to my tantrums and gave me the special weapon. And a good thing, too. I would exchange that for Madhusudan's Sudarshan Chakra. It was the perfect plan. With the discus, I could be a war hero.

"I have no objection."

Whoopee! My mind jumped somersaults in joy.

"If you can handle the Chakra, please feel free to take it with you," Madhusudan said without a trace of disappointment or anger as he raised his hand invoking the Chakra to appear. Lo and behold, the mystical and most powerful Sudarshan Chakra was rotating on the little finger of his right hand, shimmering and dazzling like a lightning streak.

He released it with his index finger . . . for me to hold. I raised my index finger to catch it when it came zipping in my direction. The discus slowed down as it reached me and it began to settle down on my raised finger. But as soon as it touched my finger, I was literally electrified. I couldn't handle the unlimited power of that disc. It was like trying to hold on to an avalanche of energy much bigger than my energy. I fell unconscious on the floor. When I came around, the harsh reality finally dawned on me. I was incapable of handling it. The son of Drona was incapable of handling the Sudarshan discus!

I was shattered. Turning around I saw Madhusudan staring sternly at me. I knew what he was about to ask. And I was right.

"No one has ever asked me for my discus," he pronounced, "neither my friend Arjuna, nor my brother Balaram, nor my sons Pradyumna, or Gada, or Samba. Tell me, what did you plan to do with it? What did you want the Sudarshan Chakra for?"

There was no harm in telling him my plan. "Madhusudan, I was going to take your Chakra and use it against you in the war to eliminate you."

"I do not fight against brahmans," Madhusudan Krishna replied in all earnestness, "but your desire to fight will be fulfilled by Arjuna in the coming days."

I hurried back to Hastinapur. Plan A had failed. Sadly, there was no plan B. Acquiring the Sudarshan Chakra would remain a distant dream for now.

CHAPTER 23

Narada Muni:

ARJUNA, THE TOPMOST DEVOTEE

*N*arayana, Narayana! this is the only word in my dictionary that is worth remembering. This is the only name I want to chant. And I do chant the Lord's name day and night, 24/7. So much so that instead of calling me by my name Narada muni, people start chanting 'Narayana, Narayana' every time they see me. This gives me great joy as it is said that a devotee is one who reminds people of Narayana.

I am also known as the transcendental spaceman because I can travel everywhere, both in the spiritual and material world. More often than not, you will find me in the spiritual world. My favourite destination is Madhavaloka where I can meet my venerable Lord. He is kind enough to grant me entry to his abode as and when I please. The guards have standing instructions to allow me in, irrespective of where I want to go. This helps me in my job. Yes, I am self-employed and my job is to connect every living being to the Supreme Being.

One fine day, I longed to see Madhava so I headed straight to his palace in Dwarka. Within moments I was in his innermost chamber. And what did I see there? I saw that Madhava and his friend Arjuna were asleep together. I gathered they must have been chatting all night and did not realise when they got knocked out by Nidra Devi, the goddess of sleep. It was quite amusing actually to see them fallen over each other. Arjuna's legs lay sprawled over Madhava's chest. And Madhava was across the bed, falling half out. Yet, he seemed extremely blissful and comfortable. In deep slumber too. As if that was the most natural position to sleep in. My amusement soon turned to resentment when it dawned on me how disrespectfully Arjuna was sprawled with his legs on Madhava. Madhava may be kind enough to call Arjuna his friend, but he was, after all, the Supreme Personality of Godhead, deserving all awe and reverence. Unhappy with the scenario, I left quietly, without waiting to meet Madhava.

Although I left the scene in a huff, the scene refused to leave me. It constantly played on my mind. How could Arjuna exhibit this kind of inappropriate behaviour? It was not right of him. Finally, unable to take it anymore, I decided to discuss this with Madhava himself. I waited for the right moment when he was alone and presented myself to him.

After exchanging pleasantries, I kept quiet, hesitating, wondering how to broach the subject as it involved his dearest friend and devotee, Arjuna. My hesitance did not escape Madhava's sharp eye and he asked me point-blank, "Pray tell me what is on your mind. What is bothering you?"

Encouraged, I spilled my heart out.

"The other day I came to your innermost chamber to find you and Arjuna sleeping. Arjuna's legs were on your chest and you didn't seem to mind that. In my opinion, Arjuna should treat you with more respect than that."

Having said everything in a single breath, I waited for his reaction. Had I offended him by pointing a finger at Arjuna, I wondered. Or, did he agree with me?

Madhava took a deep breath and said, "I understand your concern but before you come to any conclusion, I want you to do something. On my request, please visit Arjuna once when he is asleep. And while there, inch closer to him to hear what comes out from his mouth when he breathes. Also, check his pulse. After that we can discuss this if you like."

His instruction made no sense to me. While sleeping, a person can only be snoring. What else can Arjuna do? Anyway, left with no option, I quickly travelled all the way from Dwarka to Arjuna's palace. At midnight, I entered his private room where I expected to find him asleep. Yes, he was asleep. I moved quietly towards his bed, careful not to wake him up. I moved my ears closer to hear the sounds from his mouth, chest, or wherever. To my astonishment, I could hear him exhaling the names of Madhava. With every breath that he took, he was chanting 'Krishna, Krishna'. It was very faint but there was no doubt that he was chanting Madhava's name in his sleep. If I had not been that close to him, I would have probably missed it. Next, I felt his pulse. With every rise in the pulse, I could hear a vibration that echoed 'Krishna, Krishna'. This was too much for me. Arjuna's devotion was palpable even in sleep. I cringed. I had doubted the integrity of such a devotee. I fled from there as fast as I could and returned to Dwarka, only to fall at Madhava's feet.

"Forgive me, Lord," I begged him, "I did as you instructed and saw Arjuna's level of devotion to you. I have nothing more to say."

Madhava asked me to stay on for a few days. I expected more action to happen soon. Days passed and soon the Pandavas declared war on the Kauravas. Duryodhan had refused Madhava's peace treaty and war was inevitable. The warring brothers were in a frenzy to get support for themselves from all sources possible. Shakuni advised Duryodhan to approach the Yadavas for their support. Balaram had a soft corner for Duryodhan and they wanted to capitalise on that. Duryodhan rushed to Dwarka so as to reach before Arjuna could. He would meet Madhava, the head of the Yadava clan, and ask for his support.

Duryodhan's chariot is known to be much faster than Arjuna's chariot. I had never given this piece of information any importance, until now. After reflecting on this fact, I realised that the speed of their respective chariots only reflected the mode of material nature which was predominant in them. Mode of passion is characterised by haste because such people have many desires and to fulfil those desires they are always rushing about. Those in the mode of goodness are slow and steady, thinking before acting. So obviously, Duryodhan, who was in the mode of passion (and ignorance), had a high-speed chariot that matched his desire-fulfilling spree. And Arjuna, in the mode of goodness (and transcendental goodness), thought through thoroughly before he took any action.

Thus, Duryodhan reached Dwarka well before Arjuna and was relieved to have arrived first. He wanted the support of the Yadavas at any cost. I myself was still in Dwarka and watching all of this.

He hurried to Madhava's room where he found him sleeping, covered in his yellow cloth. Although Duryodhan believed he had reached Madhava first, it was true only materially speaking. Madhava had, in fact, covered himself with *maya*, the yellow covering. He made himself inaccessible to Duryodhan; one by sleeping and two, by his maya covering.

Duryodhan found himself a seat near Madhava's head end of the bed. He found it below his dignity to sit at his feet. When Arjuna arrived, he too found Madhava sleeping and so he sat at his feet. As soon as Arjuna sat, Madhava sprang to life.

"Arjuna," he exclaimed with joy and surprise, "when did you come?"

Duryodhan was flabbergasted. Madhava had

not seen him. He muttered, "But I was here first, Madhava."

Madhava turned around, surprised to see Duryodhan as well. "But I saw Arjuna first." He said firmly. Little did Duryodhan realise that it was more important who God sees first because only when he glances, there is mercy.

Arjuna explained the reason for his coming, to ask for Madhava's support in war. Madhava asked, "What do you want? You can either choose me or my massive Narayani sena. If you choose me, remember, I will not pick up any weapon to fight. You can decide first."

For Duryodhan, the choice was a no-brainer. He definitely wanted the huge Narayani sena. What was the use of a single Madhava, that too if he was going to be without any weapon. His only anxiety was that Arjuna was given the first preference. What if he chose the sena leaving him with Madhava? That would be a disaster for the Kauravas. He fervently prayed for Arjuna to lose his presence of mind and choose Madhava instead of the obvious choice of a fully-equipped army.

I felt sorry for Duryodhan's lack of foresight.

Madhava's options were not as simple as they appeared. He was actually asking them: *do you want my opulence or do you want me. Is your heart attracted to worldly glitter and glamour or does it seek me?*

Arjuna, of course, did not go after worldly attractions. All he wanted was Madhava. For him, his world revolved around Madhava. I, of all people, had experienced this first-hand. It came as no surprise then when Arjuna chose Madhava to be by his side. He chose externally what he had always chosen internally. With that one choice, Arjuna had sealed the outcome of the war.

As soon as Duryodhan heard Arjuna's decision, he jumped with joy. His heart jumped somersaults and he thanked his blessed stars. He thought it was sheer luck that Arjuna had handed the strong army to him on a platter. Afraid that Madhava would convince Arjuna to change his mind, Duryodhan took his permission to leave and hastily left the august gathering. He had achieved what he desired and there was no point in staying further. His legs carried him out as quickly as possible.

This set me thinking. Duryodhan wanted God's opulence over God. In life, we come across people who have all possible luxuries and prosperity, which, for us, implies that God has been kind to them. But how far from the truth that is! Duryodhan had also taken with him Madhava's opulent army but what he had left behind was God himself. So, the presence of opulence simply means that one had chosen not God but God's wealth.

I couldn't help but admire Madhava's game plan. By saying he would not pick up a weapon, he had thrown a googly. Because the truth is, he did not need to pick up a weapon. He could still do anything and everything without us being aware of it. This we would know later from the story of Barbarik. Think about it. How did stalwarts like Bhishma and Drona fall? Bhishma alone could have destroyed the Pandavas. Yet, the Pandavas were victorious. It was because of the invisible hand of Madhava.

It's time now for me to leave Dwarka. *Narayana, Narayana!*

CHAPTER 24

King of Udupi:
WARRIORS NEED TO EAT TOO!

The Pandavas were on their way to Udupi. Why would they come to the little temple town of Udupi? There could be only one reason behind their visit. I was one of the very few kings who had not yet taken sides in the Great War between the two warring cousins, the Pandavas and the Kauravas. Kings from other lands had already pledged their loyalty to one of the two. But I had yet to do that. Why? Did I not want to align my forces with the noble Pandavas? Did I have a soft corner for the wicked Kauravas? Why had I not declared my intentions as yet? My ministers were getting restless with my silence, lest I make the unwise decision of being on the side of *adharma*.

The Kauravas were clearly bullying the Pandavas. Not only had they usurped their kingdom, but they were also trying to kill them. My sympathies lay all the way with the Pandavas. But there was more to the decision than simply this. I was from the land of Udupi, a land renowned as a holy place. Famous as a centre for Vedic learning and the site of two very significant temples, Sri Ananteshvar and Sri Chandramauleshvar. The people of Udupi were peace-lovers and spent all their time in spiritual pursuits. With such a religious background, fighting wars was not on my list of priorities. However, I also knew that I could not avoid it altogether. This was a do-or-die battle for the Pandavas and the future of the world rested on the outcome of the war. I could not afford to keep the Udupi army out of it. That would be shameful for a *Kshatriya*.

I had been so lost in my thoughts all day that I had even forgotten to eat. Now suddenly, I felt hunger pangs hitting me. Exactly at the same time, I had a brainwave. The hunger pangs had found a solution to my waxing dilemma. I had found a solution to participate in the war and yet not be a part of the gory bloodbath. The thought shone like an enthusiastic beam of light dispelling the blanket of gloom that had surrounded my being. I rushed to the courtroom to convene a meeting. I could feel a spring in my step and joy in my heart. I was ready for the Pandavas.

The Pandavas arrived soon. I welcomed them with great pomp and fanfare. After the formalities were done, they quickly came to the point.

"King of Udupi," began Yudhishthir, "we have come here to invite you to fight the war from our side."

And the five brothers looked at me intently, waiting for my reply.

"Venerable Princes, please hear me out," I began earnestly. I spoke sincerely and humbly.

"This war will be fought against adharma but it will be fought on *dharmic* principles." Everyone nodded.

Encouraged, I continued, "At the end of the day, soldiers from both camps must sit together and eat." Again, everyone nodded in agreement.

"I would request you to give me the task of feeding the soldiers on both sides,"

I concluded with folded hands.

Yudhishthir looked at his brothers. Finding no objection from them, he agreed to my request.

"So be it."

The Pandavas departed with their entourage as I excitedly began menu-planning for the war. It was a humungous task. I would need the best of chefs and the best of ingredients. I would need an army to cook the food that would feed both the armies!

Preparations were underway and it was time for action. Day one of the war had come to a close. Yudhishthir and Sri Krishna were sitting together for their meal and I served them personally. My greatest challenge was the quantity of food to be cooked. I had no way of knowing how many warriors would lose their lives on any given day. With each passing day, lesser quantities of food would be required. At the same time, there should be enough for the survivors. It was a complex situation. Nonetheless, I managed to make exactly the right quantity of food every day.

One day, the Pandavas came into the kitchen to ask the cooks how much food was left. To their shock, they discovered there were no leftovers. The cooks told them, "Each day our king tells us the exact number of people to cook for. Somehow, he knows how many people will die each day. And he is always right. We cook for the number he gives us and there's neither a shortage nor wastage."

Intrigued, the brothers searched me out and asked, "How is it that you know how many warriors will die each day? It's impossible. It's uncanny. How could you possibly know?"

Their astonishment at my accuracy was plainly visible.

"Nothing mystical about it," I replied humbly. Really, I had not done anything as magical as it sounded. I had simply paid attention to indications from the most important person in the war, Sri Krishna.

"Krishna loves boiled peanuts. So, every day after dinner, I give him a bowl of pre-counted peanuts. Once he has finished eating, I calculate the number of peanuts he has eaten. If he has eaten ten peanuts, I know that next day 10,000 soldiers will be killed and thus I know the number of people to cook for."

The brothers were amazed. It was Sri Krishna who was running the show and they were merely instruments in his hands. And as for me, my team and I enjoyed running the kitchen so much that after going back to Udupi, we continued this as a service. Cooking food became very much a part of Udupi culture after the war!

CHAPTER 25

A Soldier:

AND THE MAHABHARAT 'MAN OF THE MATCH' AWARD GOES TO . . .

"Who is responsible for the Pandava victory?"

This was one question doing the rounds amongst us soldiers from the Pandava camp, ever since the war ended. We belonged to the lower ranks of soldiers who were left behind in Hastinapur to safeguard the city. But once the Pandavas won the war, we were called into the war zone to help clear the dead bodies. As a soldier, I believed that the battlefield is where I belonged. Disappointed at having missed out on all the action, I was happy to be in Kurukshetra even though the war was over. With every dead body we lifted, we would speculate on who must have killed him. In this way, we imagined ourselves in the middle of all the action.

However, most of the bodies we saw were either hit by arrows or by a mace. This made us think they were either hit by Arjuna or by Bhima. Of course, everyone knows that Arjuna also wields a mace and Bhima is a good archer as well. But we naively supposed that if a warrior had arrow marks it was from Arjuna and if it was a mace, it could only be from Bhima. This sparked a debate. Who would wear the crown of victory? It divided us into two groups. One that vehemently believed that Arjuna was responsible for the win and the other firmly believing it was Bhima who steered the Pandavas to victory. Initially, this debate had started in our circle, but like a wild forest fire, it had fanned out wide.

Going by the rule-book, the credit for victory is always given to the commander-in-chief of the army. In this case, however, the commander-in-chief Dhrishtadyumna himself was dead. In fact, even during the war, Arjuna and Bhima had always been considered more important than him. The two of them together and individually had foiled the attacks of Bhishma, Drona, Karna, and other stalwarts.

Now that this fire had spread, it also reached the ears of Arjuna and Bhima. Both of them were eager to know what the verdict was. Who would get the credit for being the man of the war? Sri Krishna, who always knew what was going on inside their heads, became aware of this new but subtle raging battle. It was a war of the egos. I was sure he would know exactly what to do.

One day, he started this discussion with Sahadev.

He said, "I hear everyone around us, from domestic assistants to the soldiers, discussing only one topic. Who will get the credit for victory in war—Arjuna? Or Bhima?"

When Sri Krishna stopped at that with one eyebrow arched, Sahadeva asked, "And what is your opinion?"

"My opinion is not important," Sri Krishna replied dismissively, "when we can ask the one person who watched the entire war. We were all so busy in the activities of the war that we had no idea of who was doing what. So, none of us can really come to any conclusions. Except for this one person who has watched the entire war. He will know exactly what happened and who deserves credit."

I was really intrigued by Krishna's words. Was there indeed someone who had watched the war and who was close enough to settle this debate?

Like me, Sahadeva was curious too. "Who is this person?"

Now all the Pandavas had gathered around Sri Krishna. They were all interested in this subject. I, too, inched closer to them so as not to miss a single word from Sri Krishna's mouth. Dressed in golden yellow garments, Sri Krishna shone like the midday sun surrounded by other celestial bodies.

"It is Barbarik's head who saw the entire war," revealed Sri Krishna.

Although we all knew Barbarik was Bhima's grandson, not everyone knew how Barbarik's head had seen the war, so Sri Krishna began to narrate how it all happened.

"When Barbarik was heading towards Kurukshetra, I intercepted him, disguised as a brahman, to gauge his strength. I asked him how long he would take to fight the war if he had to fight all alone. I had asked the same question to many others like Bhishma, Drona, Karna, and Arjuna. Bhishma had said it would take him twenty days. Drona said twenty-five; Karna estimated twenty-four, and Arjuna, twenty-eight.

"Thus, I was taken aback on hearing Barbarik's answer. One minute! It was unbelievable. One minute for him as compared to twenty days for Bhishma. And he was carrying only three arrows. My head was reeling and I asked him how he proposed to do that. He showed me the three arrows which were a gift from Lord Shiva and the bow which was a gift from Agnideva. He said his first arrow would mark everything and everyone he wanted to destroy. The second would mark whatever he wanted saved. And the third would hit the respective targets and finish the job. I was sceptical about whether he could actually do what he claimed. I asked for a demonstration. I asked him to shed all the leaves from the peepul tree under which we were standing. He agreed readily.

"When he was meditating on the first arrow before releasing it, I quietly plucked a peepul leaf and covered it with my foot without his knowledge. He opened his eyes and released the arrow, which whizzed past us and zoomed on the leaves. After marking all the leaves, it came back and started hovering around my foot. I acted surprised and asked why the arrow was targeting my foot? He correctly said that there was a leaf under my foot. He advised me to lift my foot else the arrow would mark my foot.

"I was now convinced that his arrows were infallible. He could finish the war in one minute with his three deadly tools. The question was, who would he fight for? Frankly speaking, I was not prepared for his answer! He said he was duty-bound to fight for the underdogs, the weaker side. Now this was a complex answer. I started thinking of the implications. To begin with, he would side with the Pandavas because on paper, they were definitely the weaker side. But because of his presence, they would soon become stronger and then Barbarik would switch sides. In this way, he would keep oscillating between the two armies. His arrows would destroy both the armies and he would ultimately be the lone survivor in the war!

"When I realised how dangerous this person actually was, I had to trick him out of this war. Being in the disguise of a brahman, I asked him for some charity. He was immediately eager to fulfil any desire that I had. He asked me to make a request. Seeing my opportunity, I told him that I needed a very special type of charity. Barbarik readily agreed. I asked him for his head. My request completely zapped Barbarik. Who would ever ask for the head of the donor? He immediately realised that I couldn't be an ordinary person to make such an unusually bold request. Surprised, he demanded to know who I was. When I revealed my identity to him, his mood completely changed. He was willing to sacrifice his life but he had only one request. He wanted to watch the war at any cost since he would not be participating in it. I granted him the wish. When he offered his head, I mounted his head on a stick that I placed on top of a hill from where he could witness the entire battle. In return for his sacrifice, I offered him my own name. Henceforth Barbarik will be called Khatu Shyam."

Sri Krishna paused to take a breath. It was clear to us now how Barbarik saw the entire war.

The group led by Sri Krishna was now marching towards the hill where Barbarik was. I could not bear to miss out on the excitement so I followed them under the pretext of serving them. Out of kindness, they did not object.

Although he was Bhima's grandson, no one doubted his integrity. As soon as they neared him, Sri Krishna asked, "You have seen the entire war. Tell us, what exactly did you see? Who would you give credit to for winning the war?"

Barbarik's hysterical laughter took us by surprise. He was Ghatotkach's son and clearly his loud rumbling laughter revealed his dynasty. But the next moment he quietened down. He said, "O'

Merciful one, I am sure you have not come all the way to simply ask me this question. This is only an excuse. You have come here to liberate me."

He looked hard at Sri Krishna and bowed his head low. "Yes, I saw the war. But actually, there was no war. It was a game played by little children. Some people only killed those who were already dead. And they believe that they are brave hearts. That they have won the war."

This really angered Bhima. "We killed dead bodies? Don't speak in riddles. Tell us what you really saw."

"Please forgive my impudence," Barbarik pleaded, "but I saw Krishna's Sudarshan Chakra in constant motion. Whoever the Chakra killed first, was later killed again by one of you or other warriors. You have only killed those who were already dead. Would you call that heroic? It was Krishna who actually orchestrated and fought the entire war. He killed everyone but no one saw that. There is only one hero. And that is Krishna."

Barbarik's head then jumped up and disappeared into thin air. He had been liberated. Everyone present there was humbled. We all bowed down to Sri Krishna. No longer did anyone want to take credit for the victory. Arjuna remembered what Sri Krishna had told him before the war. *Be my instrument.* That's exactly what Arjuna and Bhima had been. The debate was redundant. We walked back to the camp. My respect for Sri Krishna had climbed up many notches. His loyalty to his friends and family was unmatched. He was worthy of being worshipped!

CHAPTER 26

Bird from Kurukshetra:

NO ONE IS TOO SMALL FOR GOD

It is believed that the Mahabharat war destroyed the largest number of human lives in history. But I beg to disagree. Yes! My ancestors witnessed the war and we know from stories handed down to us that it was not just humans that got killed, but us birds as well.

Let me introduce myself so you understand my story better. I am a red-wattled lapwing, a family of birds that have made Kurukshetra our home. We are incapable of perching on trees. We live on the ground. In the breeding season, we nest on the ground, sand, or grass, laying three to four eggs and making sure that they are camouflaged well. It can be very dangerous for our eggs to be lying on the ground, vulnerable to being stamped by animals, humans, and their vehicles. If anyone dares to come near our eggs, we scream out so loud that the predators flee in fear. Mongoose, crows, and kites are always searching for our eggs and are our sworn enemies. Interestingly, our sounds resemble human voices, something like 'did-he-do-it' and so we are also colloquially called by the locals as did-he-do-it bird.

The story goes that my great-great-great-grandmother lived at the time of this historical war. The story has been passed down through generations and we delightfully revel in it. One fine morning of Dwapar yuga, when my great-great-great-grandmother woke up, she was shocked to find the usually quiet tract of land that she called home buzzing with activity. And what activities! Millions and millions of soldiers, horses, and elephants had gathered in Kurukshetra. From her experience, she knew this assembly meant the beginning of a war. She had heard of the Kaurava-Pandava conflict and guessed it was a war between the two warring cousins of the same family. Being very family-centric, she felt sorry for their petty ways. If only humans would learn from us to stay together as one big family!

But her immediate concern was her eggs. Her precious eggs! Tears rolled down her cheeks because now her eggs would certainly be destroyed by the enormous army. She and her husband began screaming loudly to somehow save their babies but who would pay attention to two insignificant birds? So far, their eggs were intact. Thankfully, they had not been crushed under the wheels of massive chariots.

Even if they got smashed, who would mourn for them? Certainly not humans! They themselves were in a do-or-die situation and such trivial matters were not on their radar.

Humans, busy in their own world, engrossed in their own anxieties may ignore the existence of us birds but that does not lessen our love and attachment to our children and family. We loved our children as much as humans do. If for a king, the prince was most valuable, for us, our eggs were nothing less.

However, my great-great-great-grandparents were not too strong physically. They tried their best to scream and save their eggs but meeting no success, they had to flee to save their lives. Although they left then, they returned after some time to salvage the eggs. Their intense love for their eggs could not keep them away for too long. Mother tells me that when they returned, they saw Arjuna's Nandighosh chariot in the middle of the two armies and his handsome chariot driver speaking gravely to him. Taking the opportunity, they flew to their eggs once again.

However, the quiet came to an abrupt end with the blowing of conches and drums. Suddenly there was mayhem all around. Once again, my ancestors let out a loud cry and flew away in fear.

Now comes the interesting part where mother taught me about karma. I love to hear about karma and how karma leads to the formation of different bodies. Mother explained that karma is accountable only in human birth and only as a human can one do sadhana *bhakti*. However, because of their desires, humans can take birth in various bodies. One of those bodies could be a bird's body. A bird could have possibly been a human in another lifetime and whatever sadhana was done in that lifetime could help the bird. Based on this logic, mother felt that our ancestors took the next step.

Together, they flew up to the flag carrying a monkey and shouted at the top of their voices, "Please save us O' Lord, shelter of the helpless, friend of all, with infinite powers. Please help us! Please save our eggs from destruction. Only you can save helpless creatures like us. We beg of you, O' ocean of mercy and compassion. You are our only hope."

The two birds circumambulated the Nandighosh chariot and then left the battlefield, fearful for their lives. They did not get a chance to return during the next eighteen days of the war. They had no idea if their prayers had been heard. They had no option but to leave and so they left. They could have returned at night but there was little hope of locating their eggs.

Mother says that even the smallest of living beings is significant in the eyes of the one who shelters and maintains each and every creature in the universe. The creator hears everything. If he disregards the pleas of even one, however small, then how can he be called the almighty? The one dressed in silken yellow garments, with a peacock feather crown on his head, heard my ancestor's cries with the same intensity with which he heard Arjuna's pleas. He had raised his head slightly and seen the prayerful birds. His glance was the ultimate hope for us. He was Dinabandhu, the friend of the distressed.

If you are in trouble and still don't call out to him for help, it is really unfortunate. His very nature is to help every troubled being. He does not think of helping if we don't call out to him. But once we do, there's no way he will not help. He goes to any length to do whatever he can to save you. He somehow makes arrangements to get you out of trouble. He belongs to all and all belong to him.

The war had begun. Arjuna was showering death with his arrows. Dinabandhu's eyes and hands were extremely busy. From the corner of his eye, he saw a huge elephant coming. He instructed Arjuna with urgency, "Arjuna, I want you to carefully cut the rope of the bell hanging from this elephant so that it falls on the ground. Do it now."

Arjuna did not need to ask why. Dinabandhu instructed him and he followed it to the 'T'. An arrow shot out from his Gandiva, cut the rope to enable the huge bell to fall on the ground. The eggs of my ancestors remained safe under that massive bell. Having done so much to save the eggs, it was easy for him to time the hatching to perfection. As soon as the eggs hatched, the bell was kicked away by an animal and at that very moment, my ancestors descended to pick up their babies. What timing and synchronisation! With perfect execution. When God is alert, no one needs to worry!

CHAPTER 27

Bhima:

MY ENCOUNTER WITH THE DEADLY NARAYANA-ASTRA

"*Ashwathama is dead!*"

These words from Yudhishthir's mouth sounded the death knell for our guru Dronacharya. We Pandavas were well aware of his deep attachment to his son Ashwathama and knew that the news of his death would take away all motivation from him to fight. We were banking on this and, not surprisingly, this is exactly what happened.

However, it took a huge effort on our part to convince Yudhishthir to utter those words. He would not lie. But it was true that Ashwathama the elephant was dead. Giving that logic, Keshav and Arjuna had tried to change his mind. When that seemed to fail, I stepped in. Being older than Arjuna, Yudhishthir took me a little bit more seriously. When I also insisted that he does as Keshav said, he finally gave in.

'*Ashwathama is dead*'—these words acted as the final nail on Dronacharya's coffin. He lost all his senses. He dropped his weapons and fell on the ground like a sack of wood. Unaware that he was in the middle of a war, he looked up at the sky as if in a trance. Dhrishtadyumna, finding him defenceless, pounced upon him and in one swift stroke, cleanly cut off his head. On the afternoon of the fifteenth day of the war, Dronacharya had been killed.

With their commander-in-chief dead, the Kuru army went into a panic. The entire force quickly backtracked from the battlefield. When Ashwathama heard of his father's death, he exploded with anger. He could not bear the fact that we had deceived his father and caused his death. They had used all possible deceitful means to cheat us but they expected us to be honest! How hypocritical was that? Unable to face the loss, he vowed to kill the five of us.

Ashwathama's vow was just the kick the Kauravas needed to celebrate. There was euphoria in their camp when Ashwathama announced that he would use the Narayan-astra to kill us. Now, Narayana-astra is nothing to joke about. It is the most potent weapon ever seen. He claimed it was given to him by his father and now was the time to use it. Our spies told us his exact words, "Neither Satyaki, nor Arjuna and not even Krishna knows how to combat the Narayana-astra. I will use it and destroy all five Pandavas. Their end is near."

Although the Kauravas were jubilant at this boastful claim, only Karna remained unimpressed. Maybe he knew that Keshav himself is the origin of the Narayan-astra and there was no weapon that Keshav could not overpower. Karna kept quiet as drum-beats reverberated from the Kaurava camp.

Ashwathama released his ultimate power. As soon as he did so, the entire sky turned an eerie dark, covered with low hanging black clouds. The winds began to blow with great ferocity. It seemed that we would all be carried away in the raging storm. Mother Earth trembled in fear. The oceanic waves climbed new heights creating terror in all sea creatures. Mountain peaks began to crumble.

We were anyway in mourning. The death of our beloved guru had shattered us completely. Arjuna was blaming himself for our guru's death. I may be Bhimasena, but I did not have the strength to console my brothers. I believe we did what we had to do and everything was fair in love and war.

The Kauravas were all out now in full vigour, empowered by Ashwathama's tall claims. The Narayan-astra effect was taking over. The sky was filling up with arrows, fireballs, discs, maces, and all kinds of weapons. Our army was being reduced to ashes and we were losing our warriors continuously. Arjuna was watching indifferently. Yudhishthir barked out orders to Satyaki and Dhrishtadyumna to escape with their respective armies. Then he turned to Keshav and said, "You are our only shelter. If you can help us we will live. Else, my brothers and I will willingly surrender to the fire of the Narayana-astra."

Simultaneously, Keshav raised his voice along with his hands and addressed the entire army, "Hear me, everyone. Throw away whatever weapons you have in your possession and get off your vehicles immediately. Do it immediately; I repeat, immediately. If you are weapon-less and vehicle-less, the Narayana-astra will not attack you. It does not attack those on the ground who have no weapons with them. Only if you fight back will you be affected by its wild fury. If you wish to fight it even mentally, the Narayana-astra will not leave you and chase you till it destroys you. So, follow my instructions NOW!"

There was a mad rush as the entire Pandava army threw away their weapons and jumped off their vehicles. No one wanted to be caught in the violent fury. But I was not sure of this being an effective tactic. I only knew of one tactic, the Kshatriya tactic. Fight till the end. I would follow that principle no matter what. Keshav always came up with weird solutions that made no sense. I saw everyone doing as he said but I stayed put on my chariot.

I could hear whispers and people pointing out to me, "Look at Bhima, he is still on his chariot."

I hollered, "It is grossly wrong for a Kshatriya to throw away his weapons in the middle of a war. I will not commit this grave error. Do not throw your weapons. Stay where you are. I will take care of the Narayana-astra."

But no one was listening to me. I turned my anger to Arjuna, "Arjuna," I yelled, "do not put yourself and your dynasty to shame by throwing away your weapons. Don't you understand?"

But Arjuna answered me calmly, "Brother, my principles do not allow me to fight against mother cow, brahmans, sadhus, and the Narayana-astra."

I was left speechless but my blood was boiling. How dare he leave his Gandiva bow in the chariot and step down? I continued growling my war cries and charged ahead to attack Ashwathama. I fired all my arrows at the weapon. The more I fired, the more was the intensity of Narayana-astra. Its entire fury was now concentrated upon me. Maybe because the others had surrendered their weapons and I was the only opponent left. I could hear Ashwathama laughing deliriously. At my imminent death.

I was covered by darkness. My family, my army was no longer in my field of vision. Neither could I see my horses or my chariot driver. Everyone had disappeared. It was just me and the divine Narayana-astra, one-on-one. I would give it my best fight and die graciously like a Kshatriya. Had not Keshav told Arjuna that by dying on the battlefield, a Kshatriya attains heavenly abode?

As I was struggling to overcome the escalating attack, I heard some sounds. Someone was approaching me. Soon they were upon me. My first instinct was to use all my might and throw them on the ground. But as soon as I felt the touch, I immediately realised they were none other than Keshav and Arjuna.

Keshav was speaking, "Bhima, will you not listen to me? Are you mad? Why have you not stopped fighting in spite of my instructions to stop? If it was possible to counterattack with force, why would Arjuna surrender his bow? Do not be stubborn. Step down. Come on."

Without giving me a chance to argue, Keshav pulled me by my hand and dragged me down on the ground. Arjuna snatched my mace and deposited it in the chariot. Keshav spread himself over me as if covering me from the attack of the Narayana-astra. He was almost pinning me down like a wrestler. I calmed down. As soon as I gave up my desire to fight, the Narayana-astra too calmed down. The sky became clear. The storm gave way to clear weather. I looked behind me and saw everyone safe and sound. The entire Pandava army was lying on the battlefield paying prostrated obeisance. Keshav had saved us once again from what could have been the biggest calamity we had ever faced. Keshav smiled at me as if saying, the brain is bigger than brawn. I smiled back. I could use my brawn another time. The best thing to do in front of some problems is to humble yourself.

CHAPTER 28

Heart-felt Revelations

Flute: From Zero to Hero

The reason I have agreed to put my story on paper is to remove the many misconceptions people have about me. People know me as Murlidhar's flute. And believe me, I am not just a flute, I am Murlidhar Krishna's flute. The music I produce is not just music but a mode of communication between Radha and Murlidhar, between gopis and Murlidhar, and also between Vrajvasis and Murlidhar. Moreover, I am the only musical instrument which is all-natural with no mechanical parts. That is the secret of my melodious sound. Being closest to nature, my sound is adored by none other than the Lord of the Universe, Sri Murlidhar himself. Radha loved me too and this was the reason Murlidhar always kept me close.

My sound was also the clarion call for all gopis to assemble near him. The gopis would hear my sound and go into a trance. In fact, not only the people of Vrindavan but also its animals and trees would stand still in a trance on hearing the divine vibrations of sound from Murlidhar's lips passing through me. They would swoon in ecstasy as if under a magic spell.

We had different tunes for everything. One was to make the Yamuna flow backwards! That was fun. And one to stop the progress of the moon. No one could figure out that we were behind these naughty mystical acts. We even had a tune to mesmerise the gods and one to control Lord Anantadeva hearing which he would start swaying madly. It felt like Murlidhar and I were a team in everything we did because we were hand in glove in every prank.

I am indeed very grateful to Sri Murlidhar. My very existence has been moulded by him. I was a nobody. A mere bamboo tree on the banks of the Yamuna river. That too, unlike my contemporaries. While my contemporaries were tall and firm reaching great heights, I was stunted and bent. For a bamboo, his pride lies in his height. I was too humble and felt undeserving of growing tall. I was so bent out of humility that I was considered useless. The villagers would cut the other tall bamboo sticks but no one bothered to cut me, thinking me to be of no use. I would stand there, believing that I was good for nothing. But I had a lot of patience and faith. Faith that I would find my destination.

My faith and patience paid off when one day,

Sri Murlidhar himself arrived at the banks of the Yamuna looking for a suitable bamboo stick to make his flute. My eyes followed him. One by one he rejected all the bamboos until he finally reached me. He saw me, humble and bent and his face lit up. He had found the perfect material to carve the perfect flute. My heart flipped when I saw him smile at me. No one had ever shown me any affection until that day. I was excited. When his hand touched me, I felt an electric shock run through every fibre of my being. He gently carried me back with him. I was eventually turned into a flute that stayed always in close proximity to him.

Later I learnt why Murlidhar had selected me from so many others. He wanted a plant that was free of ego and empty inside in order to do what he wanted. He found that quality in me. I totally surrendered, more than willing to give myself to him. And for that I received the highest reward possible. I was eternally in his hands, or on his lips, or tucked safely at his waist. How lucky was I! From a rejected bamboo, I had become Sri Murlidhar's prized possession. Even the gopis were jealous of me. My journey is truly amazing and a beacon of hope for all those who think they have no purpose in life. My message to them is to have patience and faith. God has a plan for you.

Peacock: Dancing with the Lord

When I look back on my life, I feel it is a life well-lived. A bird's life is not always easy. But being a peacock made all the difference. As peacocks, we get a lot of love and attention thanks to our gorgeous plumage which outshines any other bird in creation. The plume is actually a tail which we call our train. Just before the rains, when we display our glorious plumes, it's a sight to behold and cherish. It is a show so spectacular that we have a huge audience jostling to get a glimpse of us. We also have the iconic status of being Lord Kartikeya's carrier. Thus, life as a peacock is all about dancing and being admired. A fun life, don't you think?

Let me also mention that I am the king of peacocks living on Govardhan Hill. There are lots of perks of living there. The most important being Giridhari, the wonderful cowherd boy, who comes there every day. I have heard from my sources that he is actually the Supreme Lord of the world. I am inclined to believe it since I have seen strange and wonderful things happening around him. I'm not sure if I should share it in public, but believe me, if there is a God, it's him! I have seen it with my own eyes; branches of fruit-laden trees bend to touch him and shower their fruits and flowers on him. I have also seen clouds showering rain when he simply glances up at them. I cannot reveal more . . . lest I offend Giridhari by my indiscretion. But in my opinion, the rumours of his being God are all true.

Now you may know Giridhari as the little boy with a peacock feather on his head. But he did not always wear that feather. There's a story behind it and I say this with pleasure because my family of peacocks played a central role in that. That feather on his head is because of us. Let me tell you what happened.

It was just another lazy afternoon on Govardhan hill and Giridhari was resting with his friends. The boys were taking a nap. Giridhari, by nature, was very restless. He could not stick to any one thing continuously. After being in a supine position for maybe a few minutes, he decided he had had enough rest. His naughty mind was actively cooking up his next lila. It was time to wake his gopa friends up. He picked up his flute and puckered his lips to blow out some stunning melodies. As soon as the sound wafted through the air and touched the ears of his drowsy friends, they perked up instantly. Their friend Giridhari, their life and soul Giridhari, was playing his flute. They abandoned their sleep and ran to him. Forming a circle, they danced around him joyfully. Who could resist being happy when the wonder-boy Giridhari was on his flute?

Not just the gopas—none of us could resist dancing either. Anyone with legs, two or four, sprang up to sway to the divine music. We were the closest to him and we rushed inside the circle of gopas. So the scene was like this. Giridhari was in the centre. We, the peacocks, had formed a circle around him and were dancing wildly with our train in full bloom. And the gopas were in a circle outside our circle. The outermost circle was formed by other birds and animals. Giridhari, with his sweet smile and glances, continuously encouraged us to dance more and more. And peacocks are always looking for an excuse to dance. How else can we show off our plumes? But today, we danced to our heart's content, totally overpowered by the mesmerising sounds from Giridhari's flute. Giridhari was enjoying the effect he was having on us and continued to play on and on.

Suddenly, I felt a tug at my heart and found it unbearable that Giridhari was dancing so far away from us. How I longed for Giridhari to dance with us. I looked at him with such longing that I imagined I saw Giridhari nod his head as if to say he understood what I wanted. Soon, he had transformed himself into a peacock and was dancing amongst us as one of us! Oh my God! My family and I went berserk. He increased his tempo and we danced madly. We danced wildly. We danced for hours and days together with Giridhari dancing along with us. We jumped excitedly. We flapped our wings and shouted out aloud. Some even fainted in ecstasy. It was such an unforgettable experience! We hardly knew what we were doing other than dancing purely for the pleasure of Giridhari.

I was faintly aware that everyone else, except the peacocks had stopped dancing and was frozen in one position, with their eyes transfixed on Giridhari. The flute was out of Giridhari's grasp and performing a musical symphony of its own. Soon, I became tired and stopped because I had never ever danced so much in my life. Now Giridhari remained as the lone dancer. His exuberant dance continued for days together until he finally reached a crescendo and then ended his magical performance.

I thought it was my duty, as the king of the peacocks, to thank him for the enchanting show and the once-in-a-lifetime opportunity to dance with him. I bowed to him in all humility and said, "Please accept our gratitude for the blissful festival of dance. We have experienced unlimited joys and thrills because of your kindness. Please accept a humble gift from the peacock community as a token of our thanks. I have nothing more valuable than my feathers. Please accept them and wear them on your body." With this, I shook my tail and deposited many feathers at his feet.

To my delight, Giridhari picked up a feather and lovingly placed it in his turban. Oh, how beautiful he looked now. Our eyes met and we conveyed our innermost feelings to each other in that one locked glance. Happily, we dispersed from there with memories that would go down to our generations as a legacy. We had created history. Today, the peacock feather is considered an integral part of Giridhari's identity. The feather reminds the world of his eternal beauty and wisdom. Some even say it represents the third eye of Giridhari. But for me, it will always be Giridhari's unforgettable love and affection for us which he showed in abundance on that memorable day.

Radha: Krishna's Hidden Love in his Gunja Garland

It was Diwali and I wanted to adorn myself with exquisite ornaments and look beautiful for this important festival. My gopi friends and I had decided to meet in the morning at Malyahari Kunda, a perfect place to hide from Krishna and make some pearl necklaces for ourselves. It was important that we did this in secrecy else he would surely interfere with our plans and stop us from making our necklaces. An hour passed by and there was no sign of Krishna.

We were rejoicing at the success of our plan. Said one gopi to me, "Radha, it's so much fun to hide here. Krishna and the gopas must be bewildered at being unable to find any of us." Everyone was delighted thinking of how we had outwitted them. But alas, our mirth was short-lived. Just as we were congratulating one other, we found ourselves surrounded by the cowherd gang led by Krishna.

"So here you are," Krishna said, looking into my eyes. I squirmed and looked away. He continued to stare at me. I wondered how he got to know our whereabouts. I have yet to figure out how he knows all our secrets. Does he have spies? Could any of the gopis be his spies? I looked at all my friends. They all appeared as shocked as I was. No, they couldn't be spies. I shrugged off the unpleasant thought.

"Radha, what are you doing?" Krishna demanded, bringing my attention back to him.

"Oh, nothing important, just threading a few pearls," I tried to sound casual.

Krishna came closer to look at the pearls. His face broke into a broad smile when he saw the beautiful necklaces we had strung together. I had selected some of the most gorgeous pearls from my mother's collection. When we wore these pearls, we would surely look like goddesses. I couldn't wait to wear them and flaunt them. But Krishna had other ideas which made me choke and gasp.

"Can you give them to me for my cows? My cows will also look pretty wearing them."

What? Give my exotic pearls to cows? No way. Thankfully, my friends felt the same way. Lalitha said, "Go away, Krishna. We can't give you our pearls."

"Only two necklaces please," begged Krishna, "for two of my favourite cows Harini and Harshini."

"Oh no!"

"Our pearls are too precious for your cows."

"We will not give our exotic pearls to you."

The gopis were unanimous in their opinion so Krishna walked away dejected. This was the first time that I had seen Krishna not snatching whatever he wanted from us. Usually, he demanded milk and butter from our pots. Of course, we wouldn't give it to him. And what a tantrum he would throw. He and his band of monsters would systematically destroy our pots and lap up the treasure flowing out. But today he did nothing of that sort. I was concerned.

He was not his normal self. Was something wrong? Suddenly, I felt all my enthusiasm draining away and I was drowning in a sea of anxiety. Why had he left without throwing a tantrum? I wanted to run after him and ask him but I was afraid all the gopis would make fun of me. Anyway, they teased me enough for having a soft corner for Krishna. So I controlled my urge and sat quietly.

After some time, we had another visitor. It was Madhumangal. A fat brahman boy from Krishna's camp. His appearance always tickled my funny bone and I could never stop laughing. But today I was in no mood to laugh. Today, he had come with a funny request. It was so weird that we had to cross-examine him for literally an hour to understand what he wanted. The conversation went something like this.

Madhumangal: "Krishna has sent me to get some pots of milk from you. He needs them urgently."

We Gopis: "What will he do with milk? And why should we give?"

Madhumangal: "Because you did not give him pearl necklaces for his cows, he decided to grow pearls of his own."

We Gopis: "What? Does he not know that pearls don't grow on trees? How foolish is that?"

Madhumangal: "So he asked Mother Yashoda to give him some pearls which he planted meticulously in a field. But now we want to nourish the pearl with milk so that we can get high-quality pearls."

This was really hilarious. We were all rolling on the ground holding our stomachs. Some laughed so hard that tears rolled down their cheeks. Madhumangal looked at us poker-faced. He was dead serious. He had truthfully told us everything that Krishna had done and waited patiently for us to give him the pots of milk. I guess Mother Yashoda had given him the pearls to humour him knowing fully well it was no use trying to change Krishna's mind. He never changes his mind once a decision is made.

I said, "And you really expect us to waste our milk over a project that is destined to fail? Nothing doing. Our milk is as precious as our pearls. We will not part with it. Tell Krishna we refused."

Disappointed, Madhumangal walked away. Now we were really curious as to what exactly Krishna and the gopas were doing. So we followed Madhumangal at a safe distance. He led us to an open field not far from where we were. The field was neatly tilled and planted with rows of pearls. Madhumangal told Krishna that we had refused to give milk for his pearl plants. Krishna stamped his foot in frustration. Then he said, "Never mind. The gopis will repent later when they see our pearls growing on trees. Let us go to Mother Yashoda and ask her for milk." And the boisterous band of boys departed from there.

They returned with pots full of milk, butter, and curd. They got into action, lovingly watering their plants. They did this every day. And every day we would hide and watch what was going on. After three days, to our amazement, the pearls had sprouted. We had never seen or heard of anything like this. The boys were jumping and shouting at their achievement. There was no end to their celebration. And imagine our horror when after three more days we saw medium-height trees with pearls hanging from their branches. There were pearls of all shapes and sizes. Of different hues and shades. Some glittered, some were opaque, and some matt. But all pearls nevertheless. We came out of hiding and went closer. We gasped at the beautiful pearls with our jaws literally dropping. The fragrance was all around and intoxicating us. By now, the boys had seen us. They surrounded us jubilantly, teasing and cheering at the same time.

Soon, news had spread that Krishna had grown pearls on trees and the entire village gathered to see the miraculous event. As the crowd gasped and marvelled, Krishna and his friends walked around like studs, with their heads in the clouds. Once the crowd had dispersed, they turned their attention back to us.

Krishna looked at me and arched an eyebrow. Clearly, he wanted my reaction. I stuttered, at a loss for words. "These are beautiful pearls, can we have them too?"

The moment I said this, I regretted it with all my heart and soul. I had offered Krishna the perfect opportunity to take revenge. Naturally, he refused. "These pearls are for my cows. I will give the remaining to the peacocks and monkeys. They are too beautiful to share with you."

My eyes flashed in anger. "Keep your pearls. I will grow my own pearls."

I could hear the gang laughing merrily as we

turned and ran with tearful eyes and broken hearts. We too wanted those gorgeous pearls. I headed straight to my mother and asked her for the best of her pearls. She gave them reluctantly. I had to promise that I would give them back to her. My friends did the same and we regrouped a few minutes later with hands full of pearls to plant. We set about our task of planting the pearls with great determination. We toiled hard and had mud all over our faces. Now it was the turn of the gopas and Krishna to watch us from behind the trees. They even sneered and called us copycats but we didn't care. We wanted our own pearl trees. If they could do it, so could we.

If they had nourished their plants with milk and butter, we had superior quality fresh hand-churned butter and ghee. We poured all our love and prayers into nurturing our plants. Lo and behold, we saw the pearls sprouting in less than three days. Whoopee! We jumped high up in the air shouting with delight. The boys heard the commotion and ran towards us. We showed them the sprouting plants. Krishna looked at them closely and with a smirk on his face he declared, "These are not pearls sprouting but toxic weeds."

It gave him great satisfaction to say that. Once again, we plunged to the depths of despair. How was it that his pearls grew into superior pearl plants while my pearls grew into toxic weeds? Not only was it humiliating but I had also lost all the pearls our mothers had given. We could not face anyone, neither the gopas nor our mothers. We sank to the ground, holding our faces in our hands, tears streaming down our cheeks.

The boys had made beautiful necklaces for their cows. Not only the cows but we also saw monkeys and peacocks sporting the necklaces. In short, everyone had been given those pearls except us. We looked at our pearl trees. They did not have pearls but small red seeds. On closer examination, we found they were gunja seeds. I had heard that gunja seeds are poisonous. Krishna was right after all. We had ended up nurturing the poisonous gunja plant. We were defeated. However, I could not see Krishna anywhere. That was good because I dreaded his non-stop teasing. Bracing myself for the worst, I tried to find him.

Soon enough, I spotted him coming towards me. I noticed he was wearing a garland made of gunja seeds. My heart skipped a beat. The seeds were poisonous. What if they harmed him in some way? I ran towards him to remove the garland and throw it away but he stopped my hand midway.

With his voice choking, he said, "These gunja berries are far superior to my pearls. You know why? Because they have been nurtured by your loving efforts. My pearls are nothing compared to these. Still, I hope you will accept this small gift from me."

He extended his hand in which he held a red velvet box with my name engraved on it. It was a work of art, no less. Clutching it excitedly, I opened it. I was over the moon to see a stupendous glittering pearl necklace. I touched it to see if it was real or yet another trick. It seemed real. His eyes were telling me to wear it. I picked it up and put it around my neck. It felt wonderful. I was wearing his pearls and he was wearing my gunja berries. In fact, he wore the gunja berries garland all the time after that. The red berries stood out beautifully against his bluish-black skin. He treasured it more than anything else in the world. And it gave me great joy because it always reminded me of his sensitivity and love for all those who are dear to him. I pray that everyone has a friend like Krishna who makes life wonderful.

Panchjanya: My Journey from the Hands of a Demon to God

Where do I begin to tell the story of my life? Mine has been a life full of excitement. I have lived in an ocean, I have housed a demon, I have witnessed kidnapping, I have been rescued by the Parampurush Sri Krishna himself and my sound is capable of vibrating and reverberating all over the world. Phew! What a journey. Intrigued, aren't you? And wondering who is this person who has seen so much and done so much?

Well, I am Sri Krishna's conch, Panchajanya, which he holds in his left hand. But I have not always been with Sri Krishna. My story begins in Prabhasa Ocean, where a demon called Panchajana lived inside me for safety. But wait, there is yet another story before that.

This goes back to the time when Sri Krishna

and Balaram were being trained in all possible ways in their guru Sandipani muni's ashram in Ujjain. They were such geniuses that they learnt all the arts and sciences in sixty-four days and sixty-four nights. Looking at their extraordinary capacities to learn and retain, Sandipani muni knew for sure that these were no ordinary children but Supreme God himself.

After sixty-four days, when they had completed their education, Krishna and Balaram asked what they could offer as 'guru *dakshina*' or fees, in today's parlance. Back then, the system was that the students offered a one-time fee according to their capacity to their guru at the completion of their education. And the guru accepted whatever was offered whole-heartedly.

Knowing their divine powers, Sandipani muni, in consultation with his wife, shared with Sri Krishna the tragedy of his life. His son, a young boy, had gone into the waters of Prabhasa Ocean and never returned. The ocean had swallowed him up. He missed his son very much and wanted him back. Learning of his teacher's painful experience, Sri Krishna was in agony. How dare the wicked ocean drown his guru's son? Seething in anger, he and Balaram immediately left for Prabhasa Ocean. There, standing on the beach, they asked the ocean to return the boy to them.

With folded hands, the ocean paid obeisance to Sri Krishna and Balaram and explained, "Although the boy drowned here, it was not my fault. A demon called Panchajana kidnapped the boy. I did not play any role in this. But I can help you find this demon. He stays deep inside my waters in the safety of a conch shell. In all probability, the boy is inside his belly."

Sri Krishna dived into the deep ocean to find the demon and save his guru's son. It did not take him even a minute to find the demon and kill him. However, there was nothing inside his belly except for the flesh of many sea animals. Disgusted, he looked around and saw me. I looked at him, afraid that he would destroy me too. However, I saw in his eyes great love and compassion. He approached me and gently picked me up with his soft hands. I felt a thrill pass through my body at his touch. It made me happy and warm all over. He tucked me inside his dhoti and emerged out of the water. I felt a sense of freedom and a sense of purpose for the first time in my life. Next Sri Krishna decided to visit Yamaraj; maybe he could give the whereabouts of the missing boy.

On reaching the house of Yamaraj, Sri Krishna remembered me and blew upon me. I can still remember the first thrill I felt when his lips touched me. While I was in a trance, Yamaraj appeared and immediately offered his humble service to him. I was not in my senses but I vaguely remember Sri Krishna asking him to return his teacher's son. Yamaraj knew that Sri Krishna being the Supreme God, his ruling was also to be held as supreme. He did as he was told and handed over the missing boy. Sri Krishna returned with the boy and handed him over to his teacher Sandipani muni as his guru dakshina.

The story ended happily not only for his teacher but also for me because my destiny changed overnight from a sinful life with a demon. I was now the revered conch held by the god of all gods, Sri Giridhari. Every time he touched me with his pink lips, I would turn a sweet pink with shyness. Mesmerised by his softness and sweetness, I vibrated and reverberated far and wide, covering the entire world.

Whenever Sri Krishna blows upon me, the wives of demons have an abortion in fear while the demigods hail it as auspicious. This is also what happened at the start of the Mahabharat war. Sri Krishna blew on me to herald the beginning of the war followed by the blowing of Devadutta by Arjuna and Paundra by Bhima. These sounds from the three conch shells created tremors in the Kaurava camp and joy in the Pandava camp. Whenever Sri Krishna puts me to his lips, I know he is signalling the end of his next opponent.

Sudarshan Chakra – How I Accepted Lord Chakradhari as My Master

It is a difficult task to narrate my story, simply because my life is not easy. I am Sudarshan Chakra, the extraordinary weapon of Chakradhari Lord Sri Krishna. I am the only weapon in existence that is mobile, moving at my own will. I do not have to be thrown; I follow instructions at my will. I have the capacity to travel several million yojanas (one yojana = eight kilometres) before you can even blink an eye. And if my target increases his speed, so do I.

I have Chakradhari's spiritual authority to devastate everything in sight. I can be tiny enough to be placed on the tip of a tulsi leaf and I can expand to encompass the entire universe too. Thus, it is difficult for me to talk about my job profile. The most difficult part is that I have to be mentally in tune with Chakradhari's will so that I can act upon his wishes. Any carelessness on my part and I will misinterpret his desire. Not that it has ever happened. I am always on high alert, resting on the little finger of his right hand.

As soon as he wishes to destroy someone or something, I get into action and do the needful. I pursue my target till my mission is accomplished. You may have heard of Chakradhari using me to destroy Shishupal. I was also the one who pursued Durvas muni when he insulted King Ambarish, a devotee of my Lord. In the Mahabharat war, I covered the sky to mislead Jayadratha into thinking that it was sunset. When Chakradhari held the Govardhan hill, I was roaming around the Govardhan hill drying up all the water that would fall off the hill ensuring that the

Vrajvasis below the mountain did not get wet and that the water did not flow into the sheltered area. I don't remember any instance where I failed to complete my task. After destroying the evil target, I find my way back to my Lord Chakradhari, wherever he may be. Other than my destructive nature, I am also known for some positive qualities like knowledge, vision, and upholding righteousness. The evil tremble at my sight, while the good rejoice when I arrive.

You may be wondering about my origin, and how I was fortunate enough to end up in Lord Chakradhari's right hand. There are many theories floating around.

One story relates to the daughter of Vishwakarma, the architect of the gods. His daughter was married to the Sun and because of the Sun's scorching brilliance, she was never able to go close to him. When she complained about this, the dutiful father reduced the intensity of the Sun by trimming part of the Sun's brilliance. The dust obtained by trimming his edges were used to make three objects. One was the flying vehicle Pushpak Viman. Another was a *trishula*, which he gifted to Lord Shiva, and the third was me, the Sudarshan

Chakra. However, the story mentioned in the *Mahabharat* seems more relevant as to how I was given to Lord Chakradhari.

Once Agni was in the middle of a bad bout of indigestion. Indigestion for Agni meant that he could not be his normal fiery self. His flames halved in intensity and size. He had continuously guzzled ghee for twelve long years thanks to a marathon yagya performed by King Swetaketu. And the result was the indigestion. Brahma suggested he eat the Khandava fire as a cure to his indigestion. The Khandava forest had hundreds of healing herbs that when consumed could cure the indigestion of Agni instantly. The forest was also home to many dangerous demons and blazing the forest would help kill two birds with one stone. The demons would get destroyed and Agni would get cured.

The cure, though it initially appeared to be simple, turned out to be a nightmare because of Indra. Every time Agni lit a fire in the forest, Indra would send his rain clouds to extinguish it. Not because of any enmity between Indra and Agni but because Indra was trying to help his demonic friend Takshak (a snake) and his family from dying in the forest.

A disappointed and frustrated Agni approached Arjuna and Chakradhari who happened to be walking around in that vicinity to help him in the war against Indra. Since Arjuna had taken a vow that he would help every needy person who came to him, he readily agreed. But he told Agni to provide him with high-quality weapons such as a bow and arrows along with a chariot so that he could counteract a formidable opponent like Indra.

Agni thought about what he could procure and then agreed to it. Varuna, the ocean god, owed him a favour and Agni would ask him for his bow. He would give Arjuna his own chariot which moved at the speed of thought. And for Chakradhari, the most appropriate weapon was me, the Sudarshan Chakra. In the past, he had slain many a demon in the avatar of Vishnu using me. So Agni procured me and delivered me to Giridhari along with the Gandiva bow and Agniratha. This is how I was once again perched on the little finger of my master and Lord Chakradhari. I was home.

Of course, Arjuna went on to help Agni and the Khandava forest was reduced to ashes. Indra had no hope of winning against a formidable duo such as Arjuna and Chakradhari. Doesn't it say in the *Bhagavad Gita* also, whenever and wherever there is Arjuna and Chakradhari, victory prevails? I am only incidental. Happy to serve my master in any which way.

Oh, did I tell you that Agni's indigestion did get cured after all, consuming the entire forest?

Kaustubha Mani – How I Came To Reside in Lord Vishnu's Garland

"He is a gem of a person" is an oft used phrase. It refers to one having the unique qualities and virtues found in a gem.

This is quite flattering for me because at least humans realise my value. As gems we are extremely precious. At the cost of sounding a tad immodest, may I say that I am one of the rarest of jewels found in heaven? I am Kaustubh mani. My contemporaries are Chinta mani, Shyamantak mani, and Rudra mani, all from heaven. My dear ones describe my colour as deep blue, like a beautiful lotus. And you will be shocked to know that my effulgence equals the sun.

Wherever I go, I bring great fortune, luxury, and opulence . . . beyond the imagination.

In comparison, Chinta mani is white and the harbinger of freedom from all sorts of worries. The Shyamantak is also blue (not a deep blue like me) and originally belonged to the Sun, whereas the Rudra mani, given to Lord Shiva by the gods, has a soft golden hue with three stripes. It is the bestower of all virtues.

As gems, we are known to have many rare qualities; we are found in limited quantities and associated with many virtues. We are unique and rare. But like I said, not all gems are equal. Literally speaking, a gem is something that is dug out of the earth or deep sea and has miraculous qualities. Let me tell you the fascinating story of my birth. It has been mentioned in the scriptures and many Vedic hymns that I was in existence even before the entire universe came into being. Awesome, isn't it?

In short, the story goes like this.

Until a point in time, the gods were fairly powerful and would easily defeat the demons whenever the demons dared to attack them. However, things changed overnight thanks to a sage called Durvas. One day, Indra, the king of the heavens, offended the exalted sage and the sage wasted no time in cursing him. He said, "Your head is full of pride because of your wealth. Let the goddess of wealth forsake you this minute."

Losing Lakshmi spelt doom for the gods. It meant that overnight, they lost their strength and fortune. The next time the demons invaded heaven, the weakened gods lost against them and Indra had to hide, abandoning his kingdom. He sought Vishnu's help in facing this humiliating state of affairs. Vishnu suggested he take the diplomatic route by forging an alliance with the demons in sharing the nectar of immortality, which could be obtained by jointly churning the ocean. But this alliance was only a trick because Vishnu had assured Indra that once the nectar was obtained, there was no need to share it with the demons.

The demons agreed. It was the first time they had ever received such a proposal of working in collaboration. They were suspicious and on guard for any mischief-mongering from the gods. The Mandarachal Mountain was used as the churning rod and Vasuki, the king of serpents, was roped in for the churning. It was a tedious process, which required even Vishnu to incarnate as the turtle Kurma in order to support the mountain on his back.

Finally, the churning yielded the desired results and many treasures popped out of the ocean. Well, all but one was a treasure. It was, in fact, a poison called Halahal which could potentially contaminate the entire milky ocean. Shiva came to the rescue and opted to drink the poison to save the world. A terrified Parvati prevented the poison from entering his body and thus the poison remained in his throat. Except for this poison, everything else that resulted from the churning was a valuable treasure, distributed among the participants. And that's where I came in. I was the fourth object to come out of the ocean.

My brilliance was such that it tantalised everyone present, forcing them to shield their eyes with their hands. The question arose of my ownership, who would own me? None dared to do so, unable to bear my effulgence. Shiva suggested that I be handed over to Vishnu because only he could handle my power. Everyone agreed and I was happily transferred to him. Vishnu is especially fond of me because I am exactly what he likes in a gem . . . zero defect and no strings attached. Thus, even today, I am present on Vishnu's body in a garland worn by him.

After I appeared, I was fortunate to see the other treasures erupting from the ocean. Surabhi, the wish-fulfilling divine cow; Uchchaihshravas, the seven-headed horse; and Airavat, along with several majestic elephants had already been thrown up by the ocean. I saw the others coming out with my own eyes. The eternally beautiful Parijat flower, the divine apsaras, Varuni, the goddess and creator of alcohol (who was promptly given to the demons), and Chandra, the moon that adorns Shiva's head. I was especially ecstatic to be right there when Ramaa the goddess of fortune made an appearance and I saw the marriage of Ramaa and Vishnu. And last but not the least, emerged Dhanvantri, the doctor of the gods, holding the pot of nectar.

The stampede that occurred following the appearance of the nectar is a story for another day. But for now, I'm happy living as the crest jewel in the garland of Lord Vishnu and Lord Mukunda. I am nothing but pure consciousness of the soul, immaculate and free from all negative qualities. I have also incarnated as the Vaishnava poet-saint Kulashekhara Alwar.

About the Author

Dr Shubha Vilas is a lifestyle coach, storyteller and author. He studied patent law after completing his engineering degree but finally chose the path of a spiritual seeker. He has just completed his PhD in leadership from Valmiki Ramayana and his thesis is considered path breaking in the field of leadership studies from ancient texts.

Ramayana: The Game of Life is his bestselling series. He's also the author of Open-Eyed Meditations, Mystical Tales for a Magical Life and Perfect Love:

5.5 Ways to a Lasting Relationship. He has authored more than 30 thought-provoking books. The focus of his work is the application of scriptural wisdom in day-to-day life and addressing the needs of corporates and the youth through power-packed seminars.

He has delivered more than 6000 talks, inspiring more than 5,25,000 people, across twenty countries in the last ten years. He is also a visiting faculty at several premiere business management schools in India including the Indian Institute of Management (IIM) and Narsee Monjee Institute of Management Studies (NMIMS), Mumbai. He has also been a guest speaker at the prestigious Massachusetts Institute of Technology (MIT), Boston; Dresden International University, Germany; WITS, Johannesburg; and several centres of Indian Institute of Technology in India. He is on the advisory board of MIT Pune's online education system.

He has also spoken at Google, Microsoft, Amazon and Samsung at their world headquarters in the USA.

To know more about him, visit www.shubhavilas.com